W9-AXB-706

Casey got her beer and moved off to the side. It was then she noticed that Zeb's eyes hadn't left her.

A shiver of heat went through her because Zeb's gaze was intense. He looked at her like...like she didn't even know what. She wasn't sure she wanted to find out because what if he could see right through her?

What if he could see how much she was attracted to *him*?

This was a bad idea. She was on a date with her brand-new CEO and he was hot and funny and brooding all at once and they were drinking their chief competitor's product and...

Zeb glanced over at her as he paid for his food and shot another warm grin at her.

And she was in trouble. Big, *big* trouble.

\* \* \*

*His Illegitimate Heir* is part of the
The Beaumont Heirs series—
One Colorado family, limitless scandal!

Dear Reader,

Welcome back to Colorado! The Beaumont Heirs are one of Denver's oldest, most preeminent families. The Beaumont Heirs are the children of Hardwick Beaumont. Although he's been dead for almost a decade, Hardwick's womanizing ways—the four marriages and divorces, the ten children and uncounted illegitimate children—are still leaving ripples in the Beaumont family.

Especially now that some of those illegitimate children are revealing themselves. Zeb Richards has always known he was Hardwick Beaumont's son—but no one else did. The fact that he was unacknowledged ate away at him, and he vowed to get even with the Beaumonts, one way or the other. He finally has his birthright—the brewery and the Beaumont name. Nothing can ruin his revenge.

Except for one outspoken brewmaster. When Casey Johnson bursts into Zeb's office, she's stunned to realize that Zeb is a Beaumont. She expects him to fire her—but she doesn't expect the sparks that fly. Things heat up between Casey and Zeb—but when plans go out the window, will he stand by her or do what his father did and hide the problem?

*His Illegitimate Heir* is a sensual story about fighting for your dreams and falling in love. I hope you enjoy reading this book as much as I enjoyed writing it! Be sure to stop by sarahmanderson.com and sign up for my newsletter at eepurl.com/nv39b to join me as I say, Long Live Cowboys!

*Sarah*

# SARAH M. ANDERSON

---

# HIS ILLEGITIMATE HEIR

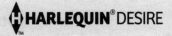

If you purchased this book without a cover you should be aware
that this book is stolen property. It was reported as "unsold and
destroyed" to the publisher, and neither the author nor the
publisher has received any payment for this "stripped book."

Recycling programs
for this product may
not exist in your area.

ISBN-13: 978-0-373-73491-7

His Illegitimate Heir

Copyright © 2016 by Sarah M. Anderson

All rights reserved. Except for use in any review, the reproduction or
utilization of this work in whole or in part in any form by any electronic,
mechanical or other means, now known or hereinafter invented, including
xerography, photocopying and recording, or in any information storage
or retrieval system, is forbidden without the written permission of the
publisher, Harlequin Enterprises Limited, 225 Duncan Mill Road,
Don Mills, Ontario M3B 3K9, Canada.

This is a work of fiction. Names, characters, places and incidents are
either the product of the author's imagination or are used fictitiously,
and any resemblance to actual persons, living or dead, business
establishments, events or locales is entirely coincidental.

This edition published by arrangement with Harlequin Books S.A.

For questions and comments about the quality of this book,
please contact us at CustomerService@Harlequin.com.

® and ™ are trademarks of Harlequin Enterprises Limited or its
corporate affiliates. Trademarks indicated with ® are registered in the
United States Patent and Trademark Office, the Canadian Intellectual
Property Office and in other countries.

HARLEQUIN®

www.Harlequin.com

Printed in U.S.A.

**Sarah M. Anderson** may live east of the Mississippi River, but her heart lies out West on the Great Plains. Sarah's book *A Man of Privilege* won an RT Reviewers' Choice Best Book Award in 2012.

Sarah spends her days having conversations with imaginary cowboys and American Indians. Find out more about Sarah's love of cowboys and Indians at sarahmanderson.com and sign up for the new-release newsletter at eepurl.com/nv39b.

### Books by Sarah M. Anderson

### Harlequin Desire

*The Nanny Plan*
*His Forever Family*
*A Surprise for the Sheikh*
*Claimed by the Cowboy*

### *The Bolton Brothers*

*Straddling the Line*
*Bringing Home the Bachelor*
*Expecting a Bolton Baby*

### *The Beaumont Heirs*

*Not the Boss's Baby*
*Tempted by a Cowboy*
*A Beaumont Christmas*
*His Son, Her Secret*
*Falling for Her Fake Fiancé*
*His Illegitimate Heir*

Visit her Author Profile page at Harlequin.com, or sarahmanderson.com, for more titles.

To Lisa Marie Perry,
who never ceases to shock and amaze me.
We'll always have Jesse Williams!

# One

"You ready for this?" Jamal asked from the front seat of the limo.

Zeb Richards felt a smile pull at the corner of his mouth. "I was born ready."

It wasn't an exaggeration. Finally, after all these years, Zeb was coming home to claim what was rightfully his. The Beaumont Brewery had—until very recently—been owned and operated by the Beaumont family. There were a hundred twenty-five years of family history in this building—history that Zeb had been deprived of.

He was a Beaumont by blood. Hardwick Beaumont was Zeb's father.

But he was illegitimate. As far as he knew, outside

of the payoff money Hardwick had given his mother, Emily, shortly after Zeb's birth, no one in the Beaumont family had ever acknowledged his existence.

He was tired of being ignored. More than that, he was tired of being denied his rightful place in the Beaumont family.

So he was finally taking what was rightfully his. After years of careful planning and sheer luck, the Beaumont Brewery now belonged to him.

Jamal snorted, which made Zeb look at him. Jamal Hitchens was Zeb's right-hand man, filling out the roles of chauffeur and bodyguard—plus, he baked a damn fine chocolate chip cookie. Jamal had worked for Zeb ever since he'd blown out his knees his senior year as linebacker at the University of Georgia, but the two of them went back much farther than that.

"You sure about this?" Jamal asked. "I still think I should go in with you."

Zeb shook his head. "No offense, but you'd just scare the hell out of them. I want my new employees intimidated, not terrified."

Jamal met Zeb's gaze in the rearview mirror and an unspoken understanding passed between the two men. Zeb could pull off intimidating all by himself.

With a sigh of resignation, Jamal parked in front of the corporate headquarters and came around to open Zeb's door. Starting right now, Zeb was a Beaumont in every way that counted.

Jamal looked around as Zeb stood and straightened the cuffs on his bespoke suit. "Last chance for backup."

"You're not nervous, are you?" Zeb wasn't. There was such a sense of rightness about this that he couldn't be nervous, so he simply wasn't.

Jamal gave him a look. "You realize you're not going to be hailed as a hero, right? You didn't exactly get this company in a way that most people might call *ethical*."

Zeb notched an eyebrow at his oldest friend. With Jamal at his back, Zeb had gone from being the son of a hairdresser to being the sole owner of ZOLA, a private equity firm that he'd founded. He'd made his millions without a single offer of assistance from the Beaumonts.

More than that, he had proven that he was better than they were. He'd outmaneuvered and outflanked them and taken their precious brewery away from them.

But taking over the family business was something he had to do himself. "Your concern is duly noted. I'll text you if I need backup. Otherwise, you'll be viewing the properties?"

They needed a place to live now that they would be based in Denver. ZOLA, Zeb's company, was still headquartered in New York—a hedge just in case his ownership of the Beaumont Brewery backfired. But buying a house here would signal to everyone that Zeb Richards wasn't going anywhere anytime soon.

Jamal realized he wasn't going to win this fight.

Zeb could tell by the way he straightened his shoulders. "Right, boss. Finest money can buy?"

"Always." It didn't really matter what the house looked like or how many bathrooms it had. All that mattered was that it was better than anyone else's. Specifically, better than any of the other Beaumonts'. "But make sure it's got a nice kitchen."

Jamal smirked at that bone of friendship Zeb threw him. "Good luck."

Zeb slid a sideways glance at Jamal. "Good luck happens when you work for it." And Zeb? He *always* worked for it.

With a sense of purpose, he strode into the corporate headquarters of the Beaumont Brewery. He hadn't called to announce his impending arrival, because he wanted to see what the employees looked like when they weren't ready to be inspected by their new CEO.

However, he was fully aware that he was an unfamiliar African American man walking into a building as if he owned it—which he did. Surely the employees knew that Zebadiah Richards was their new boss. But how many of them would recognize him?

True to form, he got plenty of double takes as he walked through the building. One woman put her hand on her phone as he passed, as if she was going to call security. But then someone else whispered something over the edge of her cubicle wall and the woman's eyes got very wide. Zeb notched an eyebrow at her and she pulled her hand away from her phone like it had burned her.

Silence trailed in his wake as he made his way toward the executive office. Zeb fought hard to keep a smile off his face. So they did know who he was. He appreciated employees who were up-to-date on their corporate leadership. If they recognized him, then they had also probably read the rumors about him.

Zebadiah Richards and his private equity firm bought failing companies, restructured them and sold them for profit. ZOLA had made him rich—and earned him a reputation for ruthlessness.

He would need that reputation here. Contrary to some of the rumors, he was not actually heartless. And he understood that the employees at this brewery had undergone the ouster of not one but two CEOs in less than a year. From his reports on the company's filings, he understood that most people still missed Chadwick Beaumont, the last Beaumont to run the brewery.

Zeb had not gotten Chadwick removed—but he had taken advantage of the turmoil that the sale of the brewery to the conglomerate AllBev had caused. And when Chadwick's temporary replacement, Ethan Logan, had failed to turn the company around fast enough, Zeb had agitated for AllBev to sell the company.

To him, of course.

But what that really meant was that he now owned a company full of employees who were scared and desperate. Employee turnover was at an all-time high. A significant percentage of top-level management had followed Chadwick Beaumont to his new company, Percheron Drafts. Many others had taken early retirement.

The employees who had survived this long were holding on by the skin of their teeth and probably had nothing left to lose. Which made them dangerous. He'd seen it before in other failing companies. Change was a constant in his world but most people hated it and if they fought against it hard enough, they could doom an entire company. When that happened, Zeb shrugged and broke the business up to be sold for its base parts. Normally, he didn't care if that happened—so long as he made a profit, he was happy.

But like he told Jamal, he was here to stay. He was a Beaumont and this was his brewery. He cared about this place and its history because it was his history, acknowledged or not. Not that he'd wanted anyone to know that this was personal—he'd kept his quest to take what was rightfully his quiet for years. That way, no one could preempt his strikes or lock him out.

But now that he was here, he had the overwhelming urge to shout, "Look at me!" He was done being ignored by the Beaumonts and he was done pretending he wasn't one of them.

Whispers of his arrival must have made it to the executive suite because when he rounded the corner, a plump older woman sitting behind a desk in front of what he assumed was the CEO's office stood and swallowed nervously. "Mr. Richards," she said in a crackly voice. "We weren't expecting you today."

Zeb nodded his head in acknowledgment. He didn't explain his sudden appearance and he didn't try to reassure her. "And you are?"

"Delores Hahn," she said. "I'm the executive assistant to the—to you." Her hands twisted nervously in front of her before she caught herself and stilled them. "Welcome to the Beaumont Brewery."

Zeb almost grinned in sympathy. His assistant was in a tough spot, but she was putting on a good face. "Thank you."

Delores cleared her throat. "Would you like a tour of the facilities?" Her voice was still a bit shaky, but she was holding it together. Zeb decided he liked Delores.

Not that he wanted her to know that right away. He was not here to make friends. He was here to run a business. "I will—after I get settled in." Then he headed for his office.

Once inside, he shut the door behind him and leaned against it. This was really happening. After years of plotting and watching and waiting, he had the Beaumont Brewery—his birthright.

He felt like laughing at the wonder of it all. But he didn't. For all he knew, Delores had her ear to the door, listening for any hint of what her new boss was like. Maniacal laughter was not a good first impression, no matter how justified it might be.

Instead, he pushed away from the door and surveyed his office. "Begin as you mean to go on," Zeb reminded himself.

He'd read about this room, studied pictures of it. But he hadn't been prepared for what it would actually feel like to walk into a piece of his family's history—to know that he belonged here, that this was his rightful place.

The building had been constructed in the 1940s by Zeb's grandfather John, soon after Prohibition had ended. The walls were mahogany panels that had been oiled until they gleamed. A built-in bar with a huge mirror took up the whole interior wall—and, if Zeb wasn't mistaken, the beer was on tap.

The exterior wall was lined with windows, hung with heavy gray velvet drapes and crowned with elaborately hand-carved woodwork that told the story of the Beaumont Brewery. His grandfather had had the conference table built in the office because it was so large and the desk was built to match.

Tucked in the far corner was a grouping of two leather club chairs and a matching leather love seat. The wagon-wheel coffee table in front of the chairs was supposed to be a wheel from the wagon that his great-great-grandfather Phillipe Beaumont had driven across the Great Plains on his way to Denver to found the brewery back in the 1880s.

The whole room screamed opulence and wealth

and history. Zeb's history. This was who he was and he would be damned if he let anyone tell him it wasn't his.

He crossed to the desk and turned on the computer—top-of-the-line, of course. Beaumonts never did anything by halves. That was one family trait they all shared.

He sat down in the leather office chair. From as far back as he could remember, his mother, Emily Richards, had told him this belonged to him. Zeb was only four months younger than Chadwick Beaumont. He should have been here, learning the business at his father's knee, instead of standing next to his mother's hairdressing chair.

But Hardwick had never married his mother—despite the fact that Hardwick had married several of his mistresses. But not Emily Richards—and for one simple reason.

Emily was black. Which made her son black.

Which meant Zeb didn't exist in the eyes of the Beaumonts.

For so long, he had been shut out of half of his heritage. And now he had the one thing that the Beaumonts had valued above all else—the Beaumont Brewery.

God, it felt good to come home.

He got himself under control. Taking possession of the brewery was a victory—but it was just the first step in making sure the Beaumonts paid for excluding him.

He was not the only Beaumont bastard Hardwick had left behind. It was time to start doing things his way. He grinned. The Beaumonts weren't going to see this coming.

He pressed the button on an antique-looking intercom. It buzzed to life and Delores said, "Yes, sir?"

"I want you to arrange a press conference for this Friday. I'm going to be announcing my plans for the brewery."

There was a pause. "Yes, sir," she said in a way that had an edge to it. "I assume you want the conference here?" Already Zeb could tell she was getting over her nervousness at his unannounced arrival.

If he had to guess, he'd say that someone like Delores Hahn had probably made the last CEO's life miserable. "Yes, on the front steps of the brewery. Oh, and Delores?"

"Yes?"

"Write a memo. Every employee needs to have an updated résumé on my desk by end of business tomorrow."

There was another pause—this one was longer. Zeb could only imagine the glare she was giving the intercom right about now. "Why? I mean—of course I'll get right on it. But is there a reason?"

"Of course there is, Delores. There is a reason behind every single thing I do. And the reason for the memo is simple. Every employee needs to reapply for their own job." He exhaled slowly, letting the tension build. "Including you."

*  *  *

"Boss?"

Casey Johnson jerked her head toward the sound of Larry's voice—which meant she smacked her forehead against the bottom of tank number fifteen. "Ow, dammit." She pushed herself out from under the tank, rubbing her head. "What?"

Larry Kaczynski was a middle-aged man with a beer gut, which was appropriate considering he brewed beer for a living. Normally, he was full of bluster and the latest stats on his fantasy football team. But today he looked worried. Specifically, he looked worried about the piece of paper in his hand. "The new guy... He's here."

"Well, good for him," Casey said, turning her attention back to her tank. This was the second new CEO in less than a year and, given recent history, he probably wouldn't make it past a couple of months. All Casey had to do was outlast him.

That, of course, was the challenge. Beer did not brew itself—although, given the attitude of the last CEO, some people thought it did.

Tank fifteen was her priority right now. Being a brewmaster was about brewing beer—but it was also about making sure the equipment was clean and functional. And right now tank fifteen wasn't either of those things.

"You don't understand," Larry sputtered before she'd rolled back under the tank. "He's been on the property for less than an hour and he's already sent this memo…"

"Larry," she said, her voice echoing against the body of the tank, "are you going to get to the point today?"

"We have to reapply for our jobs," Larry said in a rush. "By the end of the day tomorrow. I don't—Casey, you know me. I don't even have a résumé. I've worked here for the last thirty years."

Oh, for the love of everything holy… Casey pushed herself out from under the tank again and sat up. "Okay," she said in a much softer voice as she got to her feet. "Start from the beginning. What does the memo say?" Because Larry was like a canary in a coal mine. If he kept calm, the staff she was left with would also keep calm. But if Larry panicked…

Larry looked down at the paper in his hands again. He swallowed hard and Casey got the strangest sensation he was trying not to crack.

Crap. They were screwed. "It just says that by end of business tomorrow, every Beaumont Brewery employee needs to have an updated résumé on the new CEO's desk so he can decide if they get to keep their job or not."

Son of a… "Let me see."

Larry handed over the paper as if he'd suddenly discovered it was contagious, and he stepped back. "What am I going to do, boss?"

Casey scanned the memo and saw that Larry had

pretty much read verbatim. Every employee, no exceptions.

She did not have time for this. She was responsible for brewing about seven thousand gallons of beer every single day of the year on a skeleton staff of seventeen people. Two years ago, forty people had been responsible for that level of production. But two years ago, the company hadn't been in the middle of the never-ending string of upstart CEOs.

And now the latest CEO was rolling up into *her* brewery and scaring the hell out of *her* employees? This new guy thought he would tell her she had to apply for her job—the job she'd earned?

She didn't know much about this Zebadiah Richards—but he was going to get one thing straight if he thought he was going to run this company.

The Beaumont Brewery brewed beer. No beer, no brewery. And no brewmaster, no beer.

She turned to Larry, who was pale and possibly shaking. She understood why he was scared—Larry was not the brightest bulb and he knew it. That was the reason he hadn't left when Chadwick lost the company or when Ethan Logan tried to right the sinking ship.

That was why Casey had been promoted over him to brewmaster, even though Larry had almost twenty years of experience on her. He liked his job, he liked beer and as long as he got regular cost-of-living increases in his salary and a year-end bonus, he was perfectly content to spend the rest of his life right where he was. He hadn't wanted the responsibility of management.

Frankly, Casey was starting to wonder why she had. "I'll take care of this," she told him.

Surprisingly, this announcement made Larry look even more nervous. Apparently, he didn't put a lot of faith in her ability to keep her temper. "What are you going to do?"

His reaction made it clear that he was afraid she'd get fired—and then he'd be in charge. "This Richards guy and I are going to have words."

Larry fretted. "Are you sure that's the smart thing to do?"

"Probably not," she agreed. "But what's he going to do—fire the brewmaster? I don't think so, Larry." She patted him on the shoulder. "Don't worry, okay?"

Larry gave her a weak smile, but he nodded resolutely.

Casey hurried to her office and stripped off her hairnet. She knew she was no great beauty, but nobody wanted to confront a new boss in a hairnet. She grabbed her Beaumont Brewery hat and slid her ponytail through the back. And she was off, yelling over her shoulder to Larry, "See if you can get that drainage tube off—and if you can, see if you can get it flushed again. I'll be back in a bit."

She did *not* have time for this. She was already working ten- to twelve-hour days—six or seven days a week—just to keep the equipment clean and the beer flowing. If she lost more of her staff...

It wouldn't come to that. She wouldn't let it. And if it did…

Okay, so she'd promised Larry she wouldn't get fired. But what if she did? Her options weren't great, but at least she had some. Unlike Larry, she did have an updated résumé that she kept on file just in case. She didn't want to use it. She wanted to stay right here at the Beaumont Brewery and brew her favorite beer for the rest of her life.

Or at least, she had. No, if she was being honest, what she really wanted was to be the brewmaster at the old Beaumont Brewery, the one she'd worked at for the previous twelve years—the one that the Beaumont family had run. Back then the brewery had been a family business and the owners had been personally invested in their employees.

They'd even given a wide-eyed college girl the chance to do something no one else had—brew beer.

But the memo in her hand reminded her that this wasn't the same brewery. The Beaumonts no longer ran things and the company was suffering.

*She* was suffering. She couldn't remember the last time she'd strung together more than twenty-four hours of free time. She was doing the job of three people and, thanks to the hiring freeze the last CEO implemented, there was no relief in sight. And now this. She could not afford to lose another single person.

She was a thirty-two-year-old brewmaster—and a woman, at that. She'd come so far so fast. But not one of her predecessors in the illustrious history of the Beaumont Brewery had put up with quite this much crap. They'd been left to brew beer in relative peace.

She stormed to the CEO suite. Delores was behind the desk. When she saw Casey coming, the older woman jumped to her feet with surprising agility. "Casey—wait. You don't—"

"Oh, yes, I do," she said, blowing past Delores and shoving open the door to the CEO's office. "Just who the hell do you think you...are?"

# Two

Casey came to a stumbling stop. Where was he?
The desk was vacant and no one was sitting on the
leather couches.

But then a movement off to her left caught her eye
and she turned and gasped in surprise.

A man stood by the windows, looking out over the
brewery campus. He had his hands in his pockets and
his back turned to her—but despite that, everything
about him screamed power and money. The cut of
his suit fit him like a second skin and he stood with
his feet shoulder-width apart, as if he were master
of all he saw.

A shiver went through her. She was not the kind of
girl who went for power suits or the men who wore

them but something about this man—this man who was threatening her job—took her breath away. Was it the broad shoulders? Or the raw power wafting off him like the finest cologne?

And then he turned to face her and all she could see were his eyes—*green* eyes. Good Lord, those eyes—they held her gaze like a magnet and she knew her breath was gone for good.

He was, hands down, the most handsome man she'd ever seen. Everything—the power suit, the broad shoulders, the close-cropped hair and most especially the eyes—it was a potent blend that she felt powerless to resist. And this was her new boss? The man who'd sent out the memo?

He notched an eyebrow at her and let his gaze travel over her body. And any admiration she had for a good suit and nice eyes died on the vine because she knew exactly what he saw. Underneath her lab coat, she had on a men's small polo shirt with Beaumont Brewery embroidered over the chest—and she'd sweat through it because the brew room was always hot. Her face was probably red from the heat and also from the anger, and she no doubt smelled like mash and wort.

She must look like a madwoman.

A conclusion he no doubt reached on his own, because by the time he looked her in the eyes, one corner of his mouth had curved up into the kind of smile that said exactly one thing.

He thought she was a joke.

Well, he'd soon learn this was no laughing matter.

"Congratulations," he said in a voice that bordered on cold. "You're first." He lifted his wrist and looked down at a watch that, even at this distance, Casey could tell was expensive. "Thirty-five minutes. I'm impressed."

His imperious attitude poured cold water on the heat that had almost swamped her. She wasn't here to gawk at a gorgeous man. She was here to protect her workers. "Are you Richards?"

"Zebadiah Richards, yes. Your new boss," he added in a menacing tone, as if he thought he could intimidate her. Didn't he know she had so very little left to lose? "And you are?"

She'd worked in a male-dominated industry for twelve years. She couldn't be intimidated. "I'm Casey Johnson—your brewmaster." What kind of name was Zebadiah? Was that biblical? "What's the meaning of this?" She held up the memo.

Richards's eyes widened in surprise—but only for a second before he once again looked ice-cold. "Forgive me," he said in a smooth voice when Casey glared at him. "I must say that you are not what I was expecting."

Casey rolled her eyes and made no attempt to hide it. Few people expected women to like beer. Even fewer people expected women to brew beer. And with a name like Casey, everyone just assumed she was a man—and usually, they assumed she was a man like Larry. Middle-aged, beer gut—the whole nine yards. "It's not my problem if you made a set of erroneous assumptions."

The moment she said it, she realized she'd also made some erroneous assumptions herself. Because she had not anticipated that the new CEO would look quite like him. Oh, sure—the power suit was par for the course. But his hair was close-cropped to his head and his eyes… Damn, she just couldn't get past them.

He grinned—oh, Lord, that was not good. Well, it was—but in a bad way because that grin took everything hard and cold about him and warmed him up. She was certainly about to break out in another sweat.

"Indeed. Well, since you're the first person to barge into my office, I'll tell you the meaning of that memo, Ms. Johnson—although I'd hope the employees here at the brewery would be able to figure it out on their own. Everyone has to reapply for their jobs."

She welcomed his condescending tone because it pushed her from falling into the heat of his eyes and kept her focused on her task. "Is that a fact? Where'd you learn that management technique? Management 'R' Us?"

Something that almost looked like amusement flickered over his gaze and she was tempted to smile. A lot of people found her abrasive and yeah, she could rub people the wrong way. She didn't pull her punches and she wasn't about to sit down and shut up just because she was a girl and men didn't like to have their authority challenged.

What was rarer was for someone to get her sense of humor. Could this Richards actually be a real man who smiled? God, she wanted to work for a man she wouldn't have to fight every step of the way. Maybe they could get along. Maybe...

But as quickly as it had appeared, the humor was gone. His eyes narrowed and Casey thought, *You're not the only one who can be condescending.*

"The purpose is twofold, Ms. Johnson. One, I'd like to see what skill sets my employees possess. And two, I want to see if they can follow basic instructions."

So much for a sense of humor. Men as hot as he was probably weren't allowed to laugh at a joke. Pity. On the other hand, if he smiled, it might kill her with handsomeness and the only thing worse than a CEO she couldn't work with would be a CEO she lusted after.

No lusting allowed. And he was making that easier with every single thing he said.

"Let me assure you, Mr. Richards, that this company did not spring fully formed from your forehead yesterday. We've been brewing beer here for—"

"For over one hundred and thirty years—I know." He tilted his head to the side and gave her a long look. "And you've only been doing it for less than a year—is that correct?"

If she weren't so pissed at him, she'd have been

terrified, because that was most definitely a threat
to her job. But she didn't have time for unproductive
emotions and anger was vastly more useful than fear.

"I have—and I earned that job. But before you
question how a woman my age can have possibly
surpassed all the good ol' boys who normally brew
beer, let me tell you that it's also because all the more
experienced brewers have already left the company.
If you want to maintain a quality product line, you're
stuck with me for the foreseeable future." She waved
the memo in front of her. "And I don't have time to
deal with this crap."

But instead of doing anything any normal boss
would do when basically yelled at by an employee—
like firing her on the spot—Richards tilted his head
to one side and looked at her again and she absolutely
did not shiver when he did it. "Why not?"

"Why not what?"

"Why don't you have time to respond to a simple
administrative task?"

Casey didn't want to betray any sign of weakness
but a trickle of sweat rolled out from under her hat
and into her eye. Dammit. He better not think she
was crying. She wiped her eyes with the palm of
her hand. "Because I'm operating with a bare-bones
staff—I have been for the last nine months. I'm doing
the work of three people—we all are. We're understaffed, overworked and—"

"And you don't have time for this 'crap,' as you
so eloquently put it," he murmured.

Was that a note of sympathy? Or was he mocking her? She couldn't read him that well.

*Not yet*, a teasing voice in the back of her mind whispered. But she pushed that voice away. She wasn't interested in reading him better. "Not if you want to fulfill production orders."

"So just hire more people."

Now she gaped at him. "What?"

He shrugged, which was an impossibly smooth gesture on him. Men should not be that smooth. It wasn't good for them, she decided. And it definitely wasn't good for her. This would be so much easier if he were at least 70 percent less attractive. "Hire more people. But I want to see their résumés, too. Why let the new people off easy, right?"

This guy didn't know anything, did he? They were screwed, then. This was the beginning of the end. Now she would have to help Larry write a résumé.

"But…there's been a hiring freeze," she told him. "For the last eight months. Until we can show a profit."

Richards stepped forward and traced a finger over the top of the conference table. It was an oddly intimate motion—a caress, almost. Watching his hand move over the wood…

She broke out in goose bumps.

"Tell me, Ms. Johnson, was it Chadwick Beaumont who put on the hiring freeze? Or Ethan Logan?"

There was something about his voice that matched his caress of the conference table. Casey studied him.

She had the oddest feeling that he looked familiar but she was sure she would remember seeing him before. Who could forget those eyes? Those...everything?

"Logan did."

"Ah," he said, shifting so he wasn't silhouetted against the window anymore. More light fell on him and Casey was startled to realize that the green eyes were set against skin that wasn't light but wasn't exactly deep brown, either. His skin was warm, almost tan, and she realized he was at least partly African American. Why hadn't she seen that right away?

Well, she knew why. First off, she was mad and when she was mad, she didn't exactly pay attention to the bigger picture. She hadn't noticed the fullness to his frowning lips or the slight flare of his nostrils. Second off, his eyes had demanded her total attention. They were striking, so gorgeous, and even... familiar?

His hand was still on top of the conference table. "So what you're telling me is that the only non-Beaumont to run this company instituted a series of policies designed to cut costs and, in the process, hamstrung the operations and production?"

"Yes." There was something about the way he said *the only non-Beaumont* that threw her for a loop.

And then—maybe because now she was paying more attention—it hit her like a ton of bricks.

This guy—this Zeb Richards who wasn't quite black and wasn't quite white—he looked vaguely familiar. Something in the nose, the chin...those eyes...

He looked a little bit like Chadwick Beaumont.

Sweet merciful heavens. He *was* a Beaumont, too.

Her knees gave in to the weight of the revelation and she lurched forward to lean on the coffee table. "Oh, my God," she asked, staring at him. "You're one of them, aren't you?"

Richards snatched his hand back and put it in his pocket like he was trying to hide something. "I can neither confirm nor deny that—at least, not until the press conference on Friday." He moved away from the conference table and toward his desk.

If he was trying to intimidate her, it wasn't working. Casey followed him. He sat behind the desk— the same place she had seen Chadwick Beaumont too many times to count and, at least three times, Hardwick Beaumont. The resemblance was unmistakable.

"My God," she repeated again. "You're one of the bastards."

He leaned back in his chair and steepled his fingers. Everything about him had shut down. No traces of humor, no hints of warmth. She was staring at the coldest man she'd ever seen. "The bastards?"

"Beaumont's bastards—there were always rumors that Hardwick had a bunch of illegitimate children." She blinked. It all made sense, in a way. The Beaumonts were a notoriously good-looking group of men and women—far too handsome for their own good. And this man... He was gorgeous. But not the same kind of blond handsomeness that had marked Chad-wick and Matthew Beaumont. She knew he would stand out in a crowd of Beaumonts. Hell, he would stand out in *any* crowd. "He was your father, wasn't he?"

Richards stared at her for a long time and she got the feeling he was making some sort of decision. She didn't know what—he hadn't fired her yet but the day wasn't over.

Her mind felt like it was fizzing with informa-tion. Zeb Richards—the mysterious man who was rumored to have single-handedly driven down the brewery's stock price so he could force AllBev to sell off the company—was a Beaumont? Did Chadwick know? Was he in on it or was this something else?

One word whispered across her mind. *Revenge.*

Because up until about thirty-seven seconds ago, Beaumont's bastards had never been anything but a rumor. And now one of them had the company.

She had no idea if this was a good thing or a very, *very* bad thing.

Suddenly, Richards leaned forward and made a minute adjustment to something on his desk. "We've gotten off track. Your primary reason for barging into my office unannounced was about résumés."

She felt like a bottle of beer that had been shaken but hadn't been opened. At any second, she might ex-plode from the pressure. "Right," she agreed, collaps-ing into the chair in front of his desk. "The problem is, some of my employees have been here for twenty, thirty years and they don't have a résumé ready to go. Producing one on short notice is going to cause nothing but panic. They aren't the kind of guys who look good on paper. What matters is that they do good work for me and we produce a quality product." She took a deep breath, trying to sound managerial. "Are you familiar with our product line?"

The corner of Richard's mouth twitched. "It's beer, right?"

She rolled her eyes at him, which, surprisingly, made him grin even more. Oh, that was a bad idea, making him smile like that, because when he did, all the hard, cold edges fell away from his face. He was the kind of handsome that wasn't fair to the rest of humanity.

*Sinful.* That was what he was. And she had been too well behaved for too long.

She shivered. She wasn't sure if it had anything to do with the smile on his face or the fact that she was cooling off and her sweat-soaked shirt was now sticking to her skin. "That's correct. We brew beer here. I appreciate you giving me the go-ahead to hire more workers but that's a process that will take weeks. Training will also take time. Placing additional paperwork demands on my staff runs the risk of compromising the quality of our beer."

Richards didn't say anything. Casey cleared her throat. "You *are* interested in the beer, right?"

He gave her another one of those measured looks.

Casey sighed. She really wasn't so complicated that he had to stare at her.

"I'm interested in the beer," he finally said. "This is a family company and I'd like to keep it that way. I must say," he went on before Casey could ask about that whole "family" thing, "I certainly appreciate your willingness to defend your staff. However, I'd like to be reassured that the employees who work for this brewery not only are able to follow basic instructions," he added with a notch of his eyebrow that made Casey want to pound on something, "but have the skills to take this company in a new direction."

"A new direction? We're...still going to brew beer, right? We're not getting into electronics or apps or anything?"

"Oh, we'll be getting into apps," he said. "But I need to know if there's anyone on staff who can handle that or if I'm going to need to bring in an outside developer—you see my point, don't you? The Beaumont Brewery has been losing market share. You brew seven thousand gallons a day—but it was eleven thousand years ago. The popularity of craft breweries—and I'm including Percheron Drafts in that—has slowly eroded our sales."

*Our* sales? He was serious, she realized. He was here to run this company.

"While I understand Logan's cost-cutting measures," he, went on, oblivious to the way her mouth had dropped open, "what we need to do at this point is not to hunker down and hope for the best, but invest heavily in research and development—new products. And part of that is connecting with our audience." His gaze traveled around the room and Casey thought there was something about him that seemed…hopeful, almost.

She wanted to like her job. She wanted to like working for Zeb Richards. And if he was really talking about launching new products—new beers— well, then she might like her job again. The feeling that blossomed in her chest was so unfamiliar that it took a second to realize what it was—hope. Hope that this might actually work out.

"Part of what made the Beaumont Brewery a success was its long family traditions," Richards went on in a quiet voice. "That's why Logan failed. The employees liked Chadwick—any idiot knows that. And his brother Phillip? Phillip was the brewery's connection with our target market. When we lost both Phillip and Chadwick, the brewery lost its way."

Everything he said made sense. Because Casey had spent the last year not only feeling lost but knowing they were lost. They lost ground, they lost employees, they lost friends—they lost the knowledge and the tradition that had made them great. She was only one woman—one woman who liked to make beer. She couldn't save the company all by herself but she was doing her damnedest to save the beer.

Still, Richards had been on the job for about two hours now—maybe less. He was talking a hell of a good game, but at this point, that was all it was—

talk. All talk and sinful handsomeness, with a hearty dollop of mystery.

But action was what this company needed. His mesmerizing eyes wouldn't right this ship all by themselves.

Still, if Richards really was a Beaumont by birth—bastard or not—he just might be able to do it. She'd long ago learned to never underestimate the Beaumonts.

"So you're going to be the one to light the path?"

He stared her in the eyes, one eyebrow gently lifted. God, if she wasn't careful, she could get lost in his gaze. "I have a plan, Ms. Johnson. You let me worry about the company and you worry about the beer."

"Sounds good to me," she muttered.

She stood because it seemed like a final sort of statement. But Richards stopped her. "How many workers do you need to hire?"

"At least ten. What I need most right now is maintenance staff. I don't know how much you know about beer, but most of what I do is automated. It's making sure to push the right button at the right time and checking to make sure that things come together the right way. It doesn't take a lot of know-how to brew beer, honestly, once you have the recipes." At this statement, both of his eyebrows lifted. "But keeping equipment running is another matter. It's hot, messy work and I need at least eight people who can take a tank apart and put it back together in less than an hour."

He thought about that for a moment. "I don't mean to be rude, but is that what you were doing before you came in here?"

She rolled her eyes again. "What gave it away?"

He grinned. Casey took another step back from the desk—away from Zeb Richards smiling at her. She tried to take comfort in the fact that he probably knew exactly how lethal his grin could be. Men as gorgeous as he was didn't get through life without knowing exactly what kind of effect they had on women—and it usually made them jerks. Which was fine. Gorgeous jerks never went for women like her and she didn't bother with them, either.

But there was something in the way he was looking at her that felt like a warning.

"I'll compromise with you, Ms. Johnson. You and your staff will be excused from submitting résumés."

That didn't sound like a compromise. That sounded like she was getting everything she asked for. Which meant the other shoe was about to drop. "And?"

"Instead…" He paused and shot her another grin. This one wasn't warm and fuzzy—this one was the sharp smile of a man who'd somehow bought a company out from under the Beaumonts. Out from under his own family. "…you and your team will produce a selection of new beers for me to choose from."

That was one hell of a shoe—and it had landed right on her. "I'm sorry?"

"Your point that the skills of some of your employees won't readily translate into bullet points on a résumé is well taken. So I'd like to see their skills demonstrated in action."

She knew her mouth was open, but she didn't think she could get it closed. She gave it a shot—nope, it was still open. "I can't just…"

"You do know how to brew beer, don't you?"

He was needling her—and it was working, dammit. "Of course I know how to brew beer. I've been brewing Beaumont beer for twelve years."

"Then what's the problem?"

It was probably bad form to strangle your boss on his first day on the job. Tempting, though. "I can't just produce beer by snapping my fingers. I have to test new recipes—and some of them are not going to work—and then there's the brewing time, and I won't be able to do any of that until I get more staff hired."

"How long will it take?"

She grasped at the first number that popped into her mind. "Two months. At least. Maybe three."

"Fine. Three months to hire the workers and test some new recipes." He sat forward in his chair and dropped his gaze to the desk, as if they were done.

"It isn't that simple," she told him. "We need to get Marketing to provide us with guidance on what's currently popular and two—"

"I don't care what Marketing says." He cut her off. "This is my company and I want it to brew beers that I like."

"But I don't even know what you like." The moment the words left her mouth, she wished she could take them back. But it was too late. He fixed those eyes on her. Heat flushed down her back, warming her from the inside out. "I mean, when it comes to beer," she quickly corrected. "We've got everything on tap…" she added, trying not to blush as she motioned to the bar that ran along one side of the wall.

Richards leaned forward on his elbows as his gaze raked up and down her body again. Damn it all, he was a jerk. He only confirmed it when he opened his mouth and said, "I'd be more than happy to take some time after work and show you exactly what I like."

Well. If that was how it was going to be, he was making it a lot easier *not* to develop a crush on him. Because she had not gotten this job by sleeping her way to the top. He might be the most beautiful man she'd ever seen and those green eyes were the stuff of fantasy—but none of it mattered if he used his power as CEO to take advantage of his employees. She was good at what she did and she wouldn't let anyone take that away from her.

"Mr. Richards, you're going to have to decide what kind of Beaumont you are going to be—*if* you really are one." His eyes hardened, but she didn't back down. "Because if you're going to be a predator like your father instead of a businessman like your brother, you're going to need a new brewmaster."

Head held high, she walked out of his office and back to her own.

Then she updated her résumé.

# Three

Zeb did not have time to think about his new brewmaster's parting shot. It was, however, difficult not to think about *her*.

He'd known full well there would be pushback against the memo. He hadn't lied when he'd told her he wanted to see who could follow directions—but he also wanted to see who wouldn't and why. Because the fact was, having the entire company divert work hours to producing résumés was not an efficient use of time. And the workers who already had up-to-date résumés ready to go—well, that was because they were a flight risk.

He couldn't say he was surprised when the brewmaster was the first person to call him on it.

But he still couldn't believe the brewmaster was a young woman with fire in her eyes and a fierce instinct to protect her employees. A woman who didn't look at him like he was ripe for the picking. A woman who took one look at him—okay, maybe more than one—and saw the truth.

A young woman with a hell of a mouth on her.

Zeb pushed Casey Johnson from his mind and picked up his phone. He started scrolling through his contacts until he came to one name in particular—Daniel Lee. He dialed and waited.

"Hello?"

"Daniel—it's Zeb. Are you still in?"

There was a pause on the other end of the line. Daniel Lee was a former political operative who'd worked behind the scenes to get several incumbents defeated. He could manipulate public perception and he could drill down into data. But that wasn't why Zeb called him.

Daniel—much like Zeb—was one of *them*. Beaumont's bastards.

"Where are you?" Daniel asked, and Zeb didn't miss the way he neatly avoided the question.

"Sitting in the CEO's office of the Beaumont Brewery. I scheduled a press conference for Friday—I'd like you to be there. I want to show the whole world that they can't ignore us anymore."

There was another pause. On one level, Zeb appreciated that Daniel was methodical. Everything he did was well thought-out and carefully researched, with the data to back it up.

But on the other hand, Zeb didn't want his relationship with his brother to be one based solely on how the numbers played out. He didn't know Daniel very well—they'd met only two months ago, after Zeb had spent almost a year and thousands upon thousands of dollars tracking down two of his half brothers. But he and Daniel were family all the same and when Zeb announced to the world that he was a Beaumont and this was his brewery, he wanted his brothers by his side.

"What about CJ?" Daniel asked.

Zeb exhaled. "He's out." Zeb had tracked down two illegitimate brothers; all three of them had been born within five years of each other. Daniel was three years younger than Zeb and half-Korean.

The other brother he'd found was Carlos Julián Santino—although he now went by CJ Wesley. Unlike Zeb and Daniel, CJ was a rancher. He didn't seem to have inherited the Beaumont drive for business.

Two months ago, when the men had all met for the first time over dinner and Zeb had laid out his plan for taking control of the brewery and finally taking what was rightfully theirs, Daniel politely agreed to look at the numbers and weigh the outcomes. But CJ had said he wasn't interested. Unlike Zeb's mother, CJ's mother had married and he'd been adopted by her husband. CJ did not consider Hardwick Beau-

mont to be his father. He'd made his position clear—
he wanted nothing to do with the Beaumonts or the
brewery.

He wanted nothing to do with his brothers.

"That's unfortunate," Daniel said. "I had hoped..."

Yeah, Zeb had hoped, too. But he wasn't going to
dwell on his failures. Not when success was within
his grasp. "I need you by my side, Daniel. This is
our time. I won't be swept under the rug any longer.
We are both Beaumonts. It's not enough that I've
taken their company away from them—I need it to
do better than it did under them. And that means I
need you. This is the dawn of a new era."

Daniel chuckled. "You can stop with the hard
sell—I'm in. But I get to be the chief marketing officer, right?"

"I wouldn't have it any other way."

There was another long pause. "This had better
work," Daniel said in a menacing voice.

Which made Zeb grin. "It already has."

It was late afternoon before Zeb was able to get
a tour of the facilities. Delores, tablet in hand, alter-
nated between leading the way and falling behind
him. Zeb couldn't tell if she was humoring him or
if she really was that intimidated.

The tour moved slowly because in every department, Zeb stopped and talked with the staff. He was
pleased when several managers asked to speak to him
privately and then questioned the need to have a ré-

sumé for every single person on staff—wouldn't it be better if they just turned in a report on head count? It was heartening, really. Those managers were willing to risk their necks to protect their people—while they still looked for a way to do what Zeb told them.

However, Zeb didn't want to be seen as a weak leader who changed his mind. He allowed the managers to submit a report by the deadline, but he still wanted to see résumés. He informed everyone that the hiring freeze was over but he needed to know what he had before he began to fill the empty cubicles.

As he'd anticipated after his conversation with Casey, the news that the hiring freeze was over—coupled with the announcement that he would prefer not to see his staff working ten- to twelve-hour days—bought him a considerable amount of goodwill. That was not to say people weren't still wary—they were—but the overwhelming emotion was relief. It was obvious Casey wasn't the only one doing the job of two or three people.

The brewhouse was the last stop on their tour. Zeb wasn't sure if that was because it was the logical conclusion or because Delores was trying to delay another confrontation with Casey.

Unsurprisingly, the brewhouse was warm, and emptier than he expected. He saw now what Casey had meant when she said most of the process was automated. The few men he did see wore white lab coats and hairnets, along with safety goggles. They held tablets and when Zeb and Delores passed them, they paused and looked up.

"The staffing levels two years ago?" Zeb asked again.

He'd asked that question at least five times already. Two years ago, the company had been in the capable hands of Chadwick Beaumont. They'd been turning a consistent profit and their market share was stable. That hadn't been enough for some of their board members, though. Leon Harper had agitated for the company's sale, which made him hundreds of millions of dollars. From everything Zeb had read about Harper, the man was a foul piece of humanity. But there was no way Zeb ever could've gotten control of the company without him.

Delores tapped her tablet as they walked along. The room was oddly silent—there was the low hum of machinery, but it wasn't enough to dampen the echoes from their footfalls. The noise bounced off the huge tanks that reached at least twenty feet high. The only other noise was a regular hammering that got louder the farther they went into the room.

"Forty-two," she said after several minutes. "That was when we were at peak capacity. Ah, here we are."

Delores pointed at the floor and he looked down and saw two pairs of jeans-clad legs jutting out from underneath the tank.

Delores gave him a cautious smile and turned her attention back to the legs. "Casey?"

Zeb had to wonder what Delores had thought of Casey bursting into his office earlier—and whether or not Casey had said anything on her way out. He still hadn't decided what he thought of the young woman. Because she did seem impossibly young to be in charge. But what she might have lacked in maturity she made up for with sheer grit.

She probably didn't realize it, but there were very few people in this world who would dare burst into his office and dress him down. And those who would try would rarely be able to withstand the force of his disdain.

But she had. Easily. But more than that, she'd rebuffed his exploratory offer. No, that wasn't a strong enough word for how she'd destroyed him with her parting shot.

So many women looked at him as their golden ticket. He was rich and attractive and single—he knew that. But he didn't want to be anyone's ticket anywhere.

Casey Johnson hadn't treated him like that. She'd matched him verbal barb for barb and *then* bested him, all while looking like a hot mess.

He'd be lying if he said he wasn't intrigued.

"…try it again," came a muffled voice from underneath the tank. This was immediately followed by more hammering, which, at this close range, was deafening.

Zeb fought the urge to cover his ears and Delores winced. When there was a break in the hammering, she gently tapped one of the two pairs of shoes with her toe. "Casey—Mr. Richards is here."

The person whose shoe she'd nudged started—which was followed by a dull *thunk* and someone going, "Ow, dammit. What?"

And then she slid out from under the tank. She was in a white lab coat, a hairnet and safety goggles, just like everyone else. "Hello again, Ms. Johnson."

Her eyes widened. She was not what one might call a conventional beauty—especially not in the hairnet. She had a small spiderweb scar on one cheek that was more noticeable when she was red in the face—and Zeb hadn't yet seen her *not* red in the face. It was an imperfection, but it drew his eyes to her. She was maybe four inches shorter than he was and he thought her eyes were light brown. He wasn't even sure what color her hair was—it had been under the hat in his office.

But she was passionate about beer and Zeb appreciated that.

"You again," she said in a tone that sounded intentionally bored. "Back for more?"

He almost laughed—but he didn't. He was Zeb Richards, CEO of the Beaumont Brewery. And he was not going to snicker when his brewmaster copped an attitude. Still, her manner was refreshing after a day of people bowing and scraping.

Once again, he found himself running through her parting shot. Was he like his father or like his brother? He didn't know much about either of them.

He knew his father had a lot of children—and ignored some of them—and he knew his half brother had successfully run the company for about ten years. But that was common knowledge anyone with an internet connection could find out.

Almost everyone else here—including one prone brewmaster with an attitude problem—would have known what she meant by that. But he didn't.

Not yet, anyway.

Delores looked shocked. "Casey," she hissed in warning. "I'm giving Mr. Richards a tour of the facilities. Would you like to show him around the tanks?"

For a moment, Casey looked contrite in the face of Delores's scolding and Zeb got the feeling Delores had held the company together longer than anyone else.

But the moment was short. "Can't. The damned tank won't cooperate. I'm busy. Come back tomorrow." And with that, she slid right back under the tank. Before either he or Delores could say anything else, that infernal hammering picked up again. This time, he was sure it was even louder.

Delores turned to him, looking stricken. "I apologize, Mr. Richards. I—"

Zeb held up a hand to cut her off. Then he nudged the shoes again. This time, both people slid out. The other person was a man in his midfifties. He looked panic-stricken. Casey glared up at Zeb. *"What."*

"You and I need to schedule a time to go over the product line and discuss ideas for new launches."

She rolled her eyes, which made Delores gasp in horror. "Can't you get someone from Sales to go over the beer with you?"

"No, I can't," he said coldly. It was one thing to let her get the better of him in the privacy of his office but another thing entirely to let her run unchallenged in front of staff. "It has to be you, Ms. Johnson. If you want to brew a new beer that matches my tastes, you should actually know what my tastes are. When can this tank be back up and running?"

She gave him a dull look. "It's hard to tell, what with all the constant interruptions." But then she notched an eyebrow at him, the corner of her mouth curving into a delicate grin, as if they shared a private joke.

He did some quick mental calculating. They didn't have to meet before Friday—getting the press conference organized had to be his first priority. But by next week he needed to be working toward a new product line.

However, he was also aware that the press conference was going to create waves. It would be best to leave Monday open. "Lunch, Tuesday. Plan accordingly."

For just one second, he thought she would argue with him. Her mouth opened and she looked like she was spoiling for a fight. But then she changed her mind. "Fine. Tuesday. Now if you'll excuse me," she added, sliding back out of view.

"I'm so sorry," Delores repeated as they hurried away from the hammering. "Casey is…"

Zeb didn't rush into the gap. He was curious what the rest of the company thought of her.

He was surprised to realize *he* admired her. It couldn't be easy keeping the beer flowing—especially not as a young woman. She had to be at least twenty years younger than nearly every other man he'd seen in the brewhouse. But she hadn't let that stop her.

Because she was, most likely, unstoppable.

He hoped the employees thought highly of her. He needed people like her who cared for the company and the beer. People who weren't constrained by what they were or were not supposed to be.

Just like he wasn't.

"She's young," Delores finished.

Zeb snorted. Compared to his assistant, almost everyone would be.

"But she's very good," Delores said with finality.

"Good." He had no doubt that Casey Johnson would fight him at every step. "Make sure HR fast-tracks her hires. I want her to have all the help she needs."

He was looking forward to this.

# Four

"Thank you all for joining me today," Zeb said, looking out at the worried faces of his chief officers, vice presidents and departmental heads. They were all crammed around the conference table in his office. They had twenty minutes until the press conference was scheduled to start and Zeb thought it was best to give his employees a little warning.

Everyone looked anxious. He couldn't blame them. He'd made everyone surrender their cell phones when they'd come into the office and a few people looked as if they were going through withdrawal. But he wasn't about to run the risk of someone preempting his announcement.

Only one person in the room looked like she knew

what was coming next—Casey Johnson. Today she also looked like a member of the managerial team, Zeb noted with an inward smile. Her hair was slicked back into a neat bun and she wore a pale purple blouse and a pair of slacks. The change from the woman who'd stormed into his office was so big that if it hadn't been for the faint spiderweb scar on her cheek, Zeb wouldn't have recognized her.

"I'm going to tell you the same thing that I'm going to tell the press in twenty minutes," Zeb said. "I wanted to give you advance warning. When I make my announcement, I expect each and every one of you to look supportive. We're going to present a unified force. Not only is the Beaumont Brewery back, but it's going to be better than ever." He glanced at Casey. She notched an eyebrow at him and made a little motion with her hands that Zeb took to mean *Get on with it.*

So he did. "Hardwick Beaumont was my father."

As expected, the entire room shuddered with a gasp, followed by a rumbling murmur of disbelief. With amusement, Zeb noted that Casey stared around the room as if everyone else should have already realized the truth.

She didn't understand how unusual she was. No one had ever looked at him and seen the Beaumont in him. All they could see was a black man from Atlanta. Very few people ever bothered to look past that, even when he'd started making serious money.

But she had.

Some of the senior employees looked grim but not surprised. Everyone else seemed nothing but shocked. And the day wasn't over yet. When the murmur had subsided, Zeb pressed on.

"Some of you have met Daniel Lee," Zeb said, motioning to Daniel, who stood near the door. "In addition to being our new chief marketing officer, Daniel is also one of Hardwick's sons. So when I tell the reporters," he went on, ignoring the second round of shocked murmurs, "that the Beaumont Brewery is back in Beaumont hands, I want to know that I have your full support. I've spent the last week getting to know you and your teams. I know that Chadwick Beaumont, my half brother," he added, proud of the way he kept his voice level, "ran this company with a sense of pride and family honor and I'm making this promise to you, here, in this room—we will restore the Beaumont pride and we will restore the honor to this company. My last name may not be Beaumont, but I am one nonetheless. Do I have your support?"

Again, his eyes found Casey's. She was looking at him and then Daniel—no doubt looking for the family resemblance that lurked beneath their unique racial heritages.

Murmurs continued to rumble around the room, like thunder before a storm. Zeb waited. He wasn't going to ask a second time, because that would denote weakness and he was never weak.

"Does Chadwick know what you're doing?"

Zeb didn't see who asked the question, but from

the voice, he guessed it was one of the older people in the room. Maybe even someone who had once worked not only for Chadwick but for Hardwick, as well. "He will shortly. At this time, Chadwick is a competitor. I wish him well, as I'm sure we all do, but he's not coming back. This is my company now. Not only do I want to get us back to where we were when he was in charge of things, but I want to get us ahead of where we were. I'll be laying out the details at the press conference, but I promise you this. We will have new beers," he said, nodding to Casey, "and new marketing strategies, thanks to Daniel and his extensive experience."

He could tell he didn't have them. The ones standing were shuffling their feet and the ones sitting were looking anywhere but at him. If this had been a normal business negotiation, he'd have let the silence stretch. But it wasn't. "This was once a great place to work and I want to make it that place again. As I discussed with some of you, I've lifted the hiring freeze. The bottom line is and will continue to be important, but so is the beer."

An older man in the back stepped forward. "The last guy tried to run us into the ground."

"The last guy wasn't a Beaumont," Zeb shot back. He could see the doubt in their eyes. He didn't look the part that he was trying to sell them on.

Then Casey stood, acting far more respectable—and respectful—than the last time he had seen her. "I don't know about everyone else, but I just want to make beer. And if you say we're going to keep making beer, then I'm in."

Zeb acknowledged her with a nod of his head and looked around this room. He'd wager that there'd be one or two resignations on his desk by Monday morning. Maybe more. But Casey fixed them with a stern look and most of his employees stood up.

"All right," the older man who had spoken earlier repeated. Zeb was going to have to learn his name soon, because he clearly commanded a great deal of respect. "What do we have to do?"

"Daniel has arranged this press conference. Think of it as a political rally." Which was what Daniel knew best. The similarities were not coincidences. "I'd like everyone to look supportive and encouraging of the new plan."

"Try to smile," Daniel said, and Zeb saw nearly everyone jump in surprise. It was the first time Daniel had spoken. "I'm going to line you up and then we're going to walk out onto the front steps of the building. I'm going to group you accordingly. You are all the face of the Beaumont Brewery, each and every one of you. Try to remember that when the cameras are rolling."

Spoken like a true political consultant.

"Mr. Richards," Delores said, poking her head in the room, "it's almost time."

Daniel began arranging everyone in line as he wanted them and people went along with it. Zeb went back to his private bathroom to splash water on his face. Did he have enough support to put on a good show?

Probably.

He stared at the mirror. He *was* a Beaumont. For almost his entire life, that fact had been a secret that only three people knew—him and his parents. If his mother had so much as breathed a word about his true parentage, Hardwick would've come after her with pitchforks and torches. He would've burned her to the ground.

But Hardwick was dead and Zeb no longer had to keep his father's secrets. Now the whole world was going to know who he really was.

He walked out to find one person still in the conference room. He couldn't even be surprised when he saw it was Casey Johnson. For some reason, something in his chest unclenched.

"How did I do?" The moment the words left his mouth, he started. He didn't need her approval. He didn't even want it. But he'd asked for it anyway.

She tilted her head to one side and studied him. "Not bad," she finally allowed. "You may lose the entire marketing department."

Zeb's eyebrows jumped up. Was it because of him or because he brought in Daniel, another outsider? "You think so?"

She nodded and then sighed. "Are you sure you know what you're doing?"

"Can you keep a secret?"

"If I say yes, is that your cue to say, 'So can I'?"

Zeb would never admit to being nervous. But if he *had* been, a little verbal sparring with Ms. Johnson would have been just the thing to distract him. He gave her a measured look. "I'll take that as a no, you can't keep a secret. Nevertheless," he went on before she could protest, "I am putting the fate of this company in the hands of a young woman with an attitude problem, when any other sane owner would turn toward an older, more experienced brewmaster. I have faith in you, Ms. Johnson. Try to have a little in me."

She clearly did not win a lot of poker games. One second, she looked like she wanted to tear him a new one for daring to suggest she might have an attitude problem. But then the compliment registered and the oddest thing happened.

She blushed. Not the overheated red that he'd seen on her several times now. This was a delicate coloring of her cheeks, a kiss of light pink along her skin. "You have faith in me?"

"I had a beer last night. Since you've been in charge of brewing for the last year, I feel it's a reasonable assumption that you brewed it. So yes, I have faith in your abilities." Her lips parted. She sucked in a little gasp and Zeb was nearly overcome with the urge to lean forward and kiss her. Because she looked utterly kissable right now.

But the moment the thought occurred to him, he pushed it away. What the hell was wrong with him today? He was about to go out and face a bloodthirsty pack of reporters. Kissing anyone—least of all his brewmaster—should have been the farthest thing from his mind. Especially considering the setdown she'd given him a few days ago.

Was he like his father or his brother?

Still, he couldn't fight the urge to lean forward. Her eyes widened and her pupils darkened.

"Don't let me down," he said in a low voice.

He wasn't sure what she would say. But then the door swung open again and Daniel poked his head in.

"Ah, Ms… Johnson, is it? We're waiting on you." He looked over her head to Zeb. "Two minutes."

Ms. Johnson turned, but at the doorway, she paused and looked back. "Don't let the company down," she told him.

He hoped he wouldn't.

Casey knew she should be paying more attention to whatever Zeb was saying. Because he was certainly saying a lot of things, some of them passionately. She caught phrases like *quality beer* and *family company* but for the most part, she tuned out.

He had faith in her? That was so disconcerting that she didn't have a good response. But the thing that had really blown her mind was that she had been—and this was by her own estimation—a royal bitch during the two times they'd met previous to today.

It wasn't that no one respected her. The guys she'd worked with for the last twelve years respected her. Because she had earned it. She had shown up, day in and day out. She had taken their crap and given as good as she got. She had taken every single job they threw at her, even the really awful ones like scrubbing out the tanks. Guys like Larry respected her because they knew her.

Aside from those two conversations, Zeb Richards didn't know her at all.

Maybe what he'd said was a load of crap. After all, a guy as good-looking as he was didn't get to be where he was in life without learning how to say the right thing at the right time to a woman. And he'd already hit on her once, on that first day when she'd burst into his office. So it was entirely possible that he'd figured out the one thing she needed to hear and then said it to soften her up.

Even though she wasn't paying attention, she still knew the moment he dropped his big bomb. She felt the tension ripple among her coworkers—but that wasn't it. No, the entire corps of reporters recoiled in shock. Seconds later, they were all shouting questions.

"Can you prove that Hardwick Beaumont was your father?"

"How many more bastards are there?"

"Did you plan the takeover with Chadwick Beaumont?"

"What are your plans for the brewery now that the Beaumonts are back in charge?"

Casey studied Richards. The reporters had jumped out of their chairs and were now crowding the stage, as if being first in line meant their questions would be answered first. Even though they weren't shouting at her, she still had the urge to flee in horror.

But not Richards. He stood behind his podium and stared down at the reporters as if they were nothing more than gnats bothering him on a summer day. After a moment, the reporters quieted down. Richards waited until they returned to their seats before ignoring the questions completely and moving on with his prepared remarks.

Well, that was impressive. She glanced at the one person who had thrown her for a loop this morning—Daniel Lee. The two men stood nearly shoulder to shoulder, with Daniel just a step behind and to the right of Richards. Richards had two inches on his half brother and maybe forty pounds of what appeared to be pure muscle. The two men shouldn't have looked anything alike. Lee was clearly Asian American and Richards wasn't definitively one ethnicity or another. But despite those differences—and despite the fact that they had apparently not been raised together, like the other Beaumonts had been— there was something similar about them. The way they held their heads, their chins—not that Casey had met all of the Beaumont siblings, but apparently, they all shared the same jaw.

As Richards continued to talk about his plans for restoring the Beaumont family honor, Casey wondered where she fit in all of this.

In her time, when she'd been a young intern fresh

out of college and desperate to get her foot in the door, Hardwick Beaumont had been…well, not an old man, but an older man. He'd had a sharp eye and wandering hands. Wally Winking, the old brewmaster, whose voice still held a faint hint of a German accent even though he'd been at the brewery for over fifty years, had told her she reminded him of his granddaughter. Then he'd told her never to be alone with Hardwick. She hadn't had to ask why.

Three days ago, Richards had made a pass at her. That was something his father would have done. But today?

Today, when they'd been alone together, he'd had faith in her abilities. He made it sound like he respected her—both as a person and as a brewmaster.

And that was what made him sound like his brother Chadwick.

Oh, her father was going to have a field day with this. And then he was going to be mad at her that she hadn't warned him in advance. To say that Carl Johnson was heavily invested in her career would be like saying that NASA sometimes thought about Mars. He constantly worried that she was on the verge of losing her job—a sentiment that had only gotten stronger over the last year. Her dad was protective of his little girl, which was both sweet and irritating.

What was she going to tell her father? She hadn't told him about her confrontational first meeting with Richards—or the second one, for that matter. But

she was pretty sure she would be on the news tonight, one face in a human backdrop behind Zeb
Richards as he completely blew up everything people thought they knew about the Beaumont family
and the brewery.

Well, there was only one thing to do. As soon
as Daniel Lee gave her phone back, she had to text
her dad.

Oh, the reporters were shouting again. Richards
picked up his tablet to walk off the platform. Daniel
motioned to the people in front of her as they were
beginning to walk back up the front steps. The press
conference was apparently over. Thank God for that.

Richards appeared to be ignoring the reporters
but that only made the reporters shout louder. He'd
almost made it to the door when Natalie Baker—the
beautiful blonde woman who trafficked in local Denver gossip on her show, *A Good Morning with Natalie Baker*—physically blocked Zeb's way with her
body. And her breasts. They were really nice ones,
the kind that Casey had never had and never would.

Natalie Baker all but purred a question at Richards. "Are there more like you?" she asked, her gaze
sweeping to include Daniel in the question.

It must've been the breasts, because for the first
time, Richards went off script. "I've located one
more brother, but he's not part of this venture. Now
if you'll excuse me."

Baker looked thrilled and the rest of the crowd
started shouting questions again. *That was a dumb*

*thing to do*, Casey thought. Now everyone would have to know who the third one was and why he wasn't on the stage with Richards and Lee.

*Men.* A nice rack and they lost their little minds.

She didn't get a chance to talk to Richards again. And even if she had, what would she have said? *Nice press conference that I didn't pay attention to?* No, even she knew that was not the way to go about things.

Besides, she had her own brand of damage control to deal with. She needed to text her dad, warning him that the company would be in the news again but he shouldn't panic—her boss had faith in her. Then she had to go back and warn her crew. No, it was probably too late for that. She had to reassure them that they were going to keep making beer. Then she had to start the hiring process for some new employees and she had to make sure that tank fifteen was actually working properly today...

And she had to get ready for Tuesday. She was having lunch and beer with the boss.

Which boss would show up?

# Five

Frankly, he could use a beer.

"Did you contact CJ?" Daniel asked. "He needs to be warned."

Here, in the privacy of his own office with no one but Daniel around, Zeb allowed himself to lean forward and pinch the bridge of his nose. Make that several beers.

"I did. He didn't seem concerned. As long as we keep his name and whereabouts out of it, he thinks he's unfindable."

Daniel snorted. "You found him."

"A fact of which I reminded him." Zeb knew that CJ's refusal to be a part of Zeb's vision for the brothers wasn't personal. Still, it bugged him. "I think it's safe to say that he's a little more laid-back than we are."

That made Daniel grin. "He'll come around. Eventually. Has there been any other...contact?"

"No." It wasn't that he expected the acknowledged members of the Beaumont family to storm the brewery gates and engage in a battle for the heart and soul of the family business. But while the rest of the world was engaged in furious rounds of questions and speculation, there had been radio silence from the Beaumonts themselves. Not even a *No comment*. Just...nothing.

Not that Zeb expected any of them to fall over themselves to welcome him and Daniel into the family. He didn't.

He checked his watch.

"Do you have a hot date?" Daniel asked in an offhand way.

"I'm having lunch with the brewmaster, Casey Johnson."

That got Daniel's attention. He sat up straighter. "And?"

*And she asked me if I was like my father or my brother and I didn't have an answer.*

But that wasn't what he said. In fact, he didn't say anything. Yes, he and Daniel were in this together, and yes, they were technically brothers. But there were some things he still didn't want to share. Daniel was too smart and he knew how to bend the truth to suit his purposes.

Zeb had no desire to be bent to anyone's purposes but his own. "We're going over the product line. It's hard to believe that a woman so young is the brewmaster in charge of all of our beer and I want to make sure she knows her stuff."

His phone rang. He winced inwardly—it was his mother. "I've got to take this. We'll talk later?"

Daniel nodded. "One last thing. I had four resignations in the marketing department."

Casey had not been wrong about that, either. She had a certain brashness to her, but she knew this business. "Hire whoever you want," Zeb said as he answered the call. "Hello, Mom."

"I shouldn't have to call you," his mother said, the steel in her voice sounding extra sharp today.

How much beer could one man reasonably drink at work? Zeb was going to have to test that limit today, because if there was one thing he didn't want to deal with right now, it was his mother.

"But I'm glad you did," he replied easily. "How's the salon?"

"Humph." Emily Richards ran a chain of successful hair salons in Georgia. Thanks to his careful management, Doo-Wop and Pop! had gone from being six chairs in a strip-mall storefront to fifteen locations scattered throughout Georgia and a small but successful line of hair weaves and braid accessories targeted toward the affluent African American buyer.

Zeb had done that for his mother. He'd taken her

from lower middle class, where the two of them got by on $30,000 a year, to upper class. Doo-Wop and Pop! had made Emily Richards rich and was on track to make even more profit this year.

But that *humph* told Zeb everything he needed to know. It didn't matter that he had taken his mother's idea and turned it into a hugely successful woman-owned business. All that really mattered to Emily Richards was getting revenge on the man she claimed had ruined her life.

A fact she drove home with her next statement. "Well? Did you finally take what's yours?"

It always came back to the brewery. And the way she said *finally* grated on his nerves like a steel file. Still, she was his mother. "It's really mine, Mom."

Those words should have filled him with satisfaction. He had done what he had set out to do. The Beaumont Brewery was his now.

So why did he feel so odd?

He shook it off. It had been an exceptionally long weekend, after all. As expected, his press conference had created not just waves but tsunamis that had to be dealt with. His one mistake—revealing that there was a third Beaumont bastard, unnamed and unknown—had threatened to undermine his triumphant ascension to power.

"They'll come for you," his mother intoned ominously. "Those Beaumonts can't let it rest. You watch your back."

Not for the first time, Zeb wondered if his mother

was a touch paranoid. He understood now what he hadn't when he was little—that his father had bought her silence. But more and more, she acted like his siblings would go to extreme measures to enforce that silence.

His father, maybe. But none of the research he'd done on any of his siblings had turned up any proclivities for violence.

Still, he knew he couldn't convince his mother. So he let it go.

There was a knock on the door and before he could say anything, it popped open. In walked Jamal, boxes stacked in his hands. When he saw that Zeb was on the phone, he nodded his head in greeting and moved quietly to the conference table. There he began unpacking lunch.

"I will," Zeb promised his mother. And it wasn't even one of those little white lies he told her to keep her happy. He had stirred up several hornets' nests over the last few days. It only made good sense to watch his back.

"They deserve to pay for what they did to me. And you," she added as an afterthought.

But wasn't that the thing? None of the Beaumonts who were living today had ever done anything to Zeb. They'd just…ignored him.

"I've got to go, Mom. I have a meeting that starts in a few minutes." He didn't miss the way his Southern accent was stronger. Hearing it roll off Mom's tongue made his show up in force.

"Humph," she repeated. "Love you, baby boy."

"Love you, too, Mom." He hung up.

"Let me guess," Jamal said as he spread out the four-course meal he had prepared. "She's still not happy."

"Let it go, man." But something about the conversation with his mother was bugging him.

For a long time, his mother had spoken of what the Beaumonts owed *him*. They had taken what rightfully belonged to him and it was his duty to get it back. And if they wouldn't give it to him legitimately, he would just have to take it by force.

But that was all she'd ever told him about the Beaumont family. She'd never told him anything about his father or his father's family. She'd told him practically nothing about her time in Denver—he wasn't all that sure what she had done for Hardwick back in the '70s. Every time he asked, she refused to answer and instead launched into another rant about how they'd cut him out of what was rightfully his.

He had so many questions and not enough answers. He was missing something and he knew it. It was a feeling he did not enjoy, because in his business, answers made money.

His intercom buzzed. "Mr. Richards, Ms. Johnson is here."

Jamal shot him a funny look. "I thought you said you were having lunch with your brewmaster."

Before Zeb could explain, the door opened and Casey walked in. "Good morning. I spoke with the cook in the cafeteria. She said she hadn't been asked to prepare any— Oh. Hello," she said cautiously when she caught sight of Jamal plating up what smelled like his famous salt-crusted beef tenderloin.

Zeb noted with amusement that today she was back in the unisex lab coat with Beaumont Brewery embroidered on the lapel—but she wasn't bright red or sweating buckets. Her hair was still in a ponytail, though. She was, on the whole, one of the least feminine women he'd ever met. He couldn't even begin to imagine her in a dress but somehow that made her all the more intriguing.

No, he was not going to be intrigued by her. Especially not with Jamal watching. "Ms. Johnson, this is Jamal—"

"Jamal Hitchens?"

Now it was Jamal's turn to take a step back and look at Casey with caution. "Yeah… You recognize me?" He shot a funny look over to Zeb, but he just shrugged.

He was learning what Zeb had already figured out. There was no way to predict what Casey Johnson would do or say.

"Of course I recognize you," she gushed. "You played for the University of Georgia—you were in the running for the Heisman, weren't you? I mean, until you blew your knees out. Sorry about that," she added, wincing.

Jamal was gaping down at her as if she'd peeled

off her skin to reveal an alien in disguise. "You know who I am?"

"Ms. Johnson is a woman of many talents," Zeb said, not even bothering to fight the grin. Jamal would've gone pro if it hadn't been for his knees. But it was rare that anyone remembered a distant runner-up for the Heisman who hadn't played ball in years. "I've learned it's best not to underestimate her. Ms. Johnson is my brewmaster."

It was hard to get the drop on Jamal, but one small woman in a lab coat clearly had. "What are you doing here?" Casey sniffed the air. "God, that smells good."

Honest to God, Jamal blushed. "Oh. Thank you." He glanced nervously at Zeb.

"Jamal is my oldest friend," Zeb explained. He almost added, *He's the closest thing I have to a brother*—but then he stopped himself. Even if it was true, the whole point of this endeavor with the Beaumont Brewery was to prove that he had a family whether they wanted him or not. "He is my right-hand man. One of his many talents is cooking. I asked him to prepare some of my favorites today to accompany our tasting." He turned to Jamal, whose mouth was still flopped open in shock. "What did you bring?" Zeb prodded.

"What? Oh, right. The food." It was so unusual to hear Jamal sound unsure of himself that Zeb had to stare. "It's a tasting menu," he began, sounding embarrassed about it. It was rare that Jamal's past life in sports ever intersected with his current life. Actually, Zeb couldn't remember a time when someone who hadn't played football recognized him.

Jamal ran through the menu—in addition to the salt-crusted beef tenderloin, which had been paired with new potatoes, there was a spaghetti Bolognese, a vichyssoise soup and Jamal's famous fried chicken. Dessert was flourless chocolate cupcakes dusted with powdered sugar—Zeb's favorite.

Casey surveyed the feast before her, and Zeb got the feeling that she didn't approve. He couldn't say why he thought that, because she was perfectly polite to Jamal at all times. In fact, when he tried to leave, she insisted on getting a picture with him so she could send it to her father—apparently, her father was a huge sports fan and would also know who Jamal was.

So Zeb took the photo for her and then Jamal hurried away, somewhere between flattered and uncomfortable.

And then Zeb and Casey were alone.

She didn't move. "So Jamal Hitchens is an old friend of yours?"

"Yes."

"And he's your...personal chef?"

Zeb settled into his seat at the head of the conference table. "Among other things, yes." He didn't offer up any other information.

"You don't really strike me as a sports guy," she replied.

"Come, now, Ms. Johnson. Surely you've re-searched me by now?"

Her cheeks colored again. He liked that delicate blush on her. He shouldn't, but he did. "I don't remember reading about you owning a sports franchise."

Zeb lifted one shoulder. "Who knows. Maybe I'll buy a team and make Jamal the general manager. After all, what goes together better than sports and beer?"

She was still standing near the door, as if he were an alligator that looked hungry. Finally, she asked, "Have you decided, then?"

"About what?"

He saw her swallow, but it was the only betrayal of her nerves. Well, that and the fact that she wasn't smart-mouthing him. Actually, that she wasn't saying whatever came to mind was unusual.

"About what kind of Beaumont you're going to be."

He involuntarily tensed and then let out a breath slowly. Like his father or his brother? He had no idea.

He wanted to ask what she knew—was it the same as the public image of the company? Or was there something else he didn't know? Maybe his father had secretly been the kindest man on earth. Or maybe Chadwick was just as bad as Hardwick had been. He didn't know.

What he did know was that the last time he'd seen her, he'd had the urge to kiss her. It'd been nerves, he'd decided. He'd been concerned about the press conference and Casey Johnson was the closest thing to a friendly face here—when she wasn't scowling at him. That was all that passing desire had been. Reassurance. Comfort.

He didn't feel comfortable now.

"I'm going to be a different kind of Beaumont," he said confidently because it was the only true thing he *could* say. "I'm my own man."

She thought this over. "And what kind of man is that?"

She had guts, he had to admit. Anyone else might have nodded and smiled and said, *Of course*. But not her. "The kind with strong opinions about beer."

"Fair enough." She headed for the bar.

Zeb watched her as she pulled on the tap with a smooth, practiced hand. He needed to stop being surprised at her competency. She was the brewmaster. Of course she knew how to pour beer. Tapping the keg was probably second nature to her. And there wasn't a doubt in his mind that she could also destroy him in a sports trivia contest.

But this was different from watching a bartender fill a pint glass. Watching her hands on the taps was far more interesting than it'd ever been before. She had long fingers and they wrapped around each handle with a firm, sure grip.

Unexpectedly, he found himself wondering what else she'd grip like that. But the moment the thought found its way to his consciousness, he pushed it aside. This wasn't about attraction. This was about beer.

Then she glanced up at him and a soft smile

ghosted across her lips, like she was actually glad to see him, and Zeb forgot about beer. Instead, he openly stared at her. Was she glad he was here? Was she able to look at him and see not just a hidden bastard or a ruthless businessman but…

…*him*? Did she see *him*?

Zeb cleared his throat and shifted in his seat as Casey gathered up the pint glasses. After a moment's consideration, she set down one pair of glasses in front of the tenderloin and another in front of the pasta. Zeb reached for the closest glass, but she said, "Wait! If we're going to do this right, I have to walk you through the beers."

"Is there a wrong way to drink beer?" he asked, pulling his hand back.

"Mr. Richards," she said, exasperated. "This is a tasting. We're not 'drinking beer.' I don't drink on the job—none of us do. I sample. That's all this is."

She was scolding him, he realized. He was confident that he'd never been scolded by an employee before. The thought made him laugh—which got him some serious side-eye.

"Fine," he said, trying to restrain himself. When had that become difficult to do? He was always restrained. *Always*. "We'll do this your way."

He'd told Jamal the truth. He should never underestimate Casey Johnson.

She went back behind his bar and filled more half-pint glasses, twenty in all. Each pair was placed in front of a different dish. And the whole time, she was quiet.

Silence was a negotiating tactic and, as such, one that never worked on Zeb. Except…he felt himself getting twitchy as he watched her focus on her work. The next thing he knew, he was volunteering information. "Four people in the marketing department have resigned," he announced into the silence. "You were right about that."

She shrugged, as if it were no big deal. "You gave a nice talk about family honor and a bunch of other stuff, but you didn't warn anyone that you were bringing in a new CMO. People were upset."

Was she upset? No, it didn't matter, he told himself. He wasn't in this business for the touchy-feely. He was in it to make money. Well, that and to get revenge against the Beaumonts.

So, with that firmly in mind, he said, "The position was vacant. And Daniel's brilliant when it comes to campaigns. I have no doubt the skills he learned in politics will apply to beer, as well." But even as he said it, he wondered why he felt the need to explain his managerial decisions to her.

Evidently, she wondered the same thing, as she held up her hands in surrender. "Hey, you don't have to justify it to me. Although it might have been a good idea to justify it to the marketing department."

She was probably right—but he didn't want to admit that, so he changed tactics. "How about your department? Anyone there decide I was the final straw?" As he asked it, he realized what he really wanted to know was if *she'd* decided he was the final straw.

What the hell was this? He didn't care what his employees thought about him. He never had. All he cared about was that people knew their jobs and did them well. Results—that was what he cared about. This was business, not a popularity contest.

Or it had been, he thought as Casey smirked at him when she took her seat.

"My people are nervous, but that's to be expected. The ones who've hung in this long don't like change. They keep hoping that things will go back to the way they were," she said, catching his eye. No, that was a hedge. She already *had* his eye because he couldn't stop staring at her. "Or some reasonable facsimile thereof. A new normal, maybe. But no, I haven't had anyone quit on me."

A new normal. He liked that. "Good. I don't want you to be understaffed again."

She paused and then cleared her throat. When she looked up at him again, he felt the ground shift under his feet. She was gazing at him with something he so desperately wanted to think was appreciation. Why did he need her approval so damned bad?

"Thank you," she said softly. "I mean, I get that owning the company is part of your birthright, I guess, but this place…" She looked around as her voice trailed off with something that Zeb recognized— longing.

It was as if he were seeing another woman—one younger, more idealistic. A version of Casey that must have somehow found her way to the Beaumont Brewery years ago. Had she gotten the job through her father or an uncle? An old family friend?

Or had she walked into this company and, in her normal assertive way, simply demanded a job and refused to take no for an answer?

He had a feeling that was it.

He wanted to know what she was doing here— what this place meant to her and why she'd risked so much to defend it. Because they both knew that he could have fired her already. Being without a brewmaster for a day or a week would have been a problem, but problems were what he fixed.

But he hadn't fired her. She'd pushed him and challenged him and…and he liked that. He liked that she wasn't afraid of him. Which didn't make any sense—fear and intimidation were weapons he deployed easily and often to get what he wanted, the way he wanted it. Almost every other employee in this company had backed down in the face of his memos and decrees. But not *this* employee.

Not Casey.

"Okay," she announced in a tone that made it clear she wasn't going to finish her earlier statement. She produced a tablet from her lab-coat pocket and sat to his right. "Let's get started."

They went through each of the ten Beaumont beers, one at a time. "As you taste each one," she said without looking at him, "think about the flavors as they hit your tongue."

He coughed. "The...flavors?"

She handed him a pint glass and picked up the other for herself. "Drinking beer isn't just chugging to get drunk," she said in a voice that made it sound like she was praying, almost. She held her glass up and gazed at the way the light filtered through the beer. Zeb knew he should do the same—but he couldn't. He was watching her.

"Drinking beer fulfills each of the senses. Every detail contributes to the full experience," she said in that voice that was serious yet also...wistful. "How does the color make you feel?" She brought the glass back to her lips—but she didn't drink. Instead, her eyes drifted shut as she inhaled deeply. "What does it smell like—and how do the aromas affect the taste? How does it feel in your mouth?"

Her lips parted and, fascinated, Zeb watched as she tipped the glass back and took a drink. Her eyelashes fluttered in what looked to him like complete and total satisfaction. Once she'd swallowed, she sighed. "So we'll rate each beer on a scale of one to five."

Did she have any idea how sensual she looked right now? Did she look like that when she'd been satisfied in bed? Or was it just the beer that did that to her? If he leaned over and touched his fingertips to her cheek to angle her chin up so he could press his lips against hers, would she let him?

"Mr. Richards?"

"What?" Zeb shook back to himself to find that Casey was staring at him with amusement.

"Ready?"

"Yes," he said because, once again, that was the truth. He'd thought he'd been ready to take over this company—but until right then, he hadn't been sure he was ready for someone like Casey Johnson.

They got to work, sipping each beer and rating it accordingly. Amazingly, Zeb was able to focus on the beer—which was good. He could not keep staring at his brewmaster like some love-struck puppy. He was Zeb Richards, for God's sake.

"I've always preferred the Rocky Top," Zeb told her, pointedly sampling—not drinking—the stalwart of the Beaumont product line. "But the Rocky Top Light tastes like dishwater."

Casey frowned at this and made a note on her tablet. "I'd argue with you, but you're right. However, it remains one of our bestsellers among women aged twenty-one to thirty-five and is one of our top overall sellers."

That was interesting. "It's the beer we target toward women and you don't like it?"

She looked up at him sharply and he could almost hear her snapping, *Women are not interchangeable.* But she didn't. Instead, in as polite a voice as he'd ever heard from her, she said, "People drink beer for different reasons," while she made notes. "I don't want to sacrifice taste for something as arbitrary as calorie count."

"Can you make it better?"

That got her attention. "We've used the same formula for… Well, since the '80s, I think. You'd want to mess with that?"

He didn't lean forward, no matter how much he wanted to. Instead, he kept plenty of space between them. "There's always room for improvement, don't you think? I'm not trapped by the past." But the moment he said it, he wondered how true that was. "Perhaps one of your experiments can be an improved light-beer recipe."

She held his gaze, her lips curved into a slight smile. It was disturbing how much he liked her meeting his challenges straight on like that. "I'll do that."

They went through the rest of the beers and, true to her word, Zeb couldn't have said that he'd drunk enough to even get a slight buzz. Finally, as they'd eaten the last of their cupcakes, he leaned back and said, "So what are we missing?"

She surprised him then. She picked up what was left of her Rocky Top and took a long drink. "Look—here's the thing about our current product line. It's fine. It's…serviceable."

He notched an eyebrow at her. "It gets the job done?"

"Exactly. But when we lost Percheron Drafts, we lost the IPA, the stout—the bigger beers with bolder tastes. We lost seasonal beers—the summer shandy and the fall Oktoberfest beers. What we've got now is basic. I'd love to get us back to having one or two spotlight beers that we could rotate in and out." She got a wistful look on her face. "It's hard to see that here, though."

"What do you mean?"

"I mean, look at this." She swept her hand out, encompassing the remains of their lunch. "*This*. Most people who drink our beer don't do so in the luxury of a private office with a catered four-course meal. They drink a beer at a game or on their couch, with a burger or a brat."

Suddenly, a feeling he'd gotten earlier—that she hadn't approved of the setup—got stronger. "What about you? Where do you drink your beer?"

"Me? Oh. I have season tickets to the Rockies. My dad and I go to every home game we can. Have you done that?" He shook his head. "You should. I've learned a lot about what people like just standing in line to get a beer at the game. I talk with the beer guys—that sort of thing."

"A ball game?" He must have sounded doubtful, because she nodded encouragingly. "I can get a box."

"Really?" She rolled her eyes. "That's not how people drink beer. Here. I'll tell you what—there's a game tomorrow night at seven, against the Braves. My dad can't go. You can use his ticket. Come with me and see what I mean."

He stared at her. It didn't sound like a come-on—but then, he'd never gotten quite so turned on watching another woman drink beer before. Nothing was typical when it came to this woman. "You're serious, aren't you?"

"Of course."

He had a feeling she was right. He'd spent years learning about the corporate workings of the brewery from a distance. If he was going to run this place as his own—and he was—then he needed to understand not just the employees but their customers.

Besides, the Braves were his team. And beyond that, this was a chance to see Casey outside work. Suddenly, that seemed important—vital, even. What was she like when she wasn't wearing a lab coat? He shouldn't have wanted to know. But he did anyway. "It's a da—" Casey's eyes got huge and her cheeks flushed and Zeb remembered that he wasn't having a drink with a pretty girl at a bar. He was at the brewery and he was the CEO. He had to act like it. "Company outing," he finished, as if that was what he'd meant to say all along.

She cleared her throat. "Covert market research, if you will." Her gaze flickered over his Hugo Boss suit. "And try to blend, maybe?"

He gave her a level stare, but she was unaffected. "Tomorrow at seven."

"Gate C." She gathered up her tablet. "We'll talk then."

He nodded and watched her walk out. Once the door was firmly closed behind her, he allowed himself to grin.

Whether she liked it or not, they had a date.

# Six

Casey really didn't know what to expect as she stood near the C gate at Coors Field. She'd told Richards to blend but she was having trouble picturing him in anything other than a perfectly tailored suit.

Not that she was spending a lot of time thinking about him in a perfectly tailored suit. She wasn't. Just because he was the epitome of masculine grace and style, that was no reason at all to think about her boss.

Besides, she didn't even go for guys in suits. She usually went for blue-collar guys, the kind who kicked back on the weekend with a bunch of beer to watch sports. That was what she was comfortable with, anyway. And comfort was good, right?

And anyway, even if she did go for guys in suits—which she did not—she was positive she didn't go for guys like Richards. It wasn't that he was African American. She had looked him up, and one of the few pictures of him on the internet was him standing with a woman named Emily Richards in Atlanta, Georgia, outside a Doo-Wop and Pop! Salon. It was easy to see the resemblance between them—she was clearly his mother.

No, her not going for guys like Richards had nothing to do with race and everything to do with the fact that he was way too intense for her. The way he'd stared at her over the lip of his pint glass during their tasting lunch? Intensity personified, and as thrilling as it had been, it wasn't what she needed on her time off. Really. She had enough intensity at work. That was why she always went for low-key guys—guys who were fun for a weekend but never wanted anything more than that.

Right. So it was settled. She absolutely did not go for someone like Richards in a suit. Good.

"Casey?"

Casey whipped around and found herself staring not at a businessman in a suit—and also not at someone who was blending. Zeb Richards stood before her in a white T-shirt with bright red raglan sleeves. She was vaguely aware that he had on a hat and reasonably certain that he was wearing blue jeans, but she couldn't tear her eyes away from his chest. The

T-shirt molded to his body in a way that his power suit hadn't. Her mouth went dry.

*Good God.*

That was as far as her brain got, because she tried to drag her eyes away from his chest—and made it exactly as far as his biceps.

*Sweet mother of pearl* was the last coherent thought she had as she tried to take in the magnitude of those biceps.

And when thinking stopped, she was left with nothing but her physical response. Her nipples tightened and her skin flushed—*flushed*, dammit, like she was an innocent schoolgirl confronted with a man's body for the first time. All that flushing left her shaken and sweaty and completely unable to look away. It took all of her self-control not to lean over and put a hand to that chest and feel what she was looking at. Because she'd be willing to bet a lot of money that he *felt* even better than he looked.

"...Casey?" he said with what she hoped like hell was humor in his voice. "Hello?"

"What?" Crap, she'd been caught gaping at him. "Right. Hi." Dumbly, she held up the tickets.

"Is there something wrong with my shirt?" He asked, looking down. Then he grasped the hem of the shirt and pulled it out so he could see the front, which had a graphic of the Braves' tomahawk on it. But when he did that, the neck of the shirt came down and Casey caught a glimpse of his collarbones.

She had no idea collarbones could be sexy. This

was turning out to be quite an educational evening and it had only just begun. How on earth was she going to get through the rest of it without doing something humiliating, like *drooling* on the man?

Because drooling was off-limits. Everything about him was off-limits.

This was not a date. Nope. He was her boss, for crying out loud.

"Um, no. I mean, I didn't actually figure you would show up in the opposing team's shirt." Finally—and way too late for decency's sake—she managed to look up into his face. He was smiling at her, as if he knew exactly what kind of effect he had on her. Dammit. This was the other reason she didn't go for men like him. They were too cocky for their own good.

"That's all," she went on. "You don't exactly blend." She was pretty sure she was babbling.

"I'm from Atlanta, you know." He smirked at her and suddenly there it was—a luscious Southern accent that threatened to melt her. "Who did you think I was going to root for?" His gaze swept over her and Casey felt each and every hair on her body stand at attention. "I don't have anything purple," he went on when his gaze made it back to her face with something that looked a heck of a lot like approval.

She fought the urge to stand up straighter. She would not pose for him. This was not a date. She didn't care what he thought of her appearance. "We could fix that," she told him, waving at the T-shirt sellers hawking all sorts of Rockies gear. He scrunched his nose at her. "Or not," she said with a melodramatic sigh, trying to get her wits about her. "It's still better than a suit. Come on. We need to get in if we want to grab a beer before the game starts."

He looked around. People in purple hats and T-shirts were making their way inside and he was already getting a few funny looks. "This is literally your home turf. Lead on."

She headed toward the turnstiles. Zeb made a move toward one with a shorter line, but Casey put her hand on his arm. "This one," she told him, guiding him toward Joel's line.

"Why?"

"You'll see." At this cryptic statement, Zeb gave her a hard look. Oddly enough, it didn't carry as much weight as it might have if he'd been in a tie, surrounded by all the brewery history in his office. Instead, he looked almost…adorable.

Crap, this was bad. She absolutely couldn't be thinking of Zebadiah Richards as adorable. Or hot. Or…anything.

There might have been some grumbling following that statement, but Casey decided that she probably shouldn't get into a shouting match with him before they'd even gotten inside the stadium.

The line moved quickly and then Joel said, "Casey! There's my girl."

"Hey, Joel," she said, leaning over to give the old man a quick hug.

"Where's Carl?" Joel asked, eyeing Zeb behind her.

"Union meeting. Who do you think's going to win today?" She and Joel had the same conversation at nearly every game.

"You have to ask? The Braves are weak this season." Then he noticed Richards's shirt behind her and his easy smile twisted into a grimace of disapproval. He leaned over and grabbed two of the special promotion items—bobblehead dolls of the team. "Take one to your dad. I know he collects them."

"Aw, thanks, Joel. And give my best to Martha, okay?"

Joel gave a bobblehead to Richards, as well. "Good luck, fella," he muttered.

When they were several feet away, Richards said, "I see what you mean about blending. Do you want this?" He held out the bobblehead.

"I'm good. Two is my personal limit on these things. Give it to Jamal or something." She led him over to her favorite beer vendor. "Speaking of, where is Jamal? I thought you might bring him."

Honestly, she couldn't decide if she'd wanted Jamal to be here or not. If he had been, then maybe she'd have been able to focus on *not* focusing on Zeb a little better. Three was a crowd, after all.

But still…she was glad Zeb had come alone.

This time, he held back and waited until she picked the beer line. "He's still unpacking."

"Oh?" There were about six people in front of

them. This game was going to be nowhere near a sellout. "So you really did move out here?"

"Of course." He slid her a side glance. "I said that at the press conference, you know."

They moved up a step in line. Casey decided that it was probably best not to admit that she hadn't been paying attention during the press conference. "So where are you guys at?"

"I bought a house over on Cedar Avenue. Jamal picked it out because he liked the kitchen."

Her eyes bugged out of her head. "You bought the mansion by the country club?"

"You know it?" He said it in such a casual way, as if buying the most expensive house in the Denver area were no biggie.

Well, maybe for him, it wasn't. Why was she surprised? She shouldn't have been. She wasn't. Someone like Zeb Richards would definitely plunk down nearly $10 million for a house and not think anything of it. "Yeah. My dad was hired to do some work there a couple years ago. He said it was an amazing house."

"I suppose it is." He didn't sound very convinced about this. But before Casey could ask him what he didn't like about the house, he went on, "What does your dad do? And I'm going to pay you back for his ticket. I'm sorry that I'm using it in his place."

She waved this away. "Don't worry about it. He really did have a union meeting tonight. He's an electrician. He does a lot of work in older homes—renovations and upgrading antique wiring. There's still a lot of knob-and-tube wiring in Denver, you know."

One corner of his mouth—not that she was staring at his mouth—curved up into a smile that was positively dangerous.

"What?" she said defensively—because if she didn't defend herself from that sly smile… Well, she didn't know what would happen. But it wouldn't be good.

In fact, it would be bad. The very best kind of bad.

"Nothing. I've just got to stop being surprised by you, that's all." They advanced another place in line. "What are we ordering?"

"Well, seeing as this is Coors Field, we really don't have too many options when it comes to beer. It's—shockingly—Coors."

"No!" he said in surprise. "Do they make beer?"

She stared at him. "Wait—was that a joke? Were you trying to be funny?"

That grin—oh, *hell*. "Depends. Did it work?"

No—well, yes, but *no*. No, she couldn't allow him to be a regular guy. If this "company outing" was going to stay strictly aboveboard, he could not suddenly develop a set of pecs *and* a sense of humor at the same time. She couldn't take it. "Mr. Richards—"

"Really, Casey," he said, cutting her off, "we're about to drink a competitor's beer outside of normal business hours at a game. Call me Zeb."

She was a strong woman. She was. She'd worked at the Beaumont Brewery for twelve years and during that time, she'd never once gotten involved with a coworker. She'd had to negotiate the fine line between "innocent flirting" and "sexual harassment" on too many occasions, but once she'd earned her place at the table, that had fallen away.

But this? Calling Richards by his first name? Buying beer with him at a ball game? Pointedly not staring at the way he filled out an officially licensed T-shirt? Listening to him crack jokes?

She simply wasn't that strong. This wasn't a company outing. It was starting to feel like a date.

They reached the cashier. "Casey!" Marco gave her a high five over the counter.

She could feel Zeb behind her. He wasn't touching her, but he was close enough that her skin was prickling. "Marco—what's the latest?"

"It happened, girl." Marco pointed to a neon sign over his head—one that proudly proclaimed they served Percheron Drafts.

Casey whistled. "You were right."

"I told you," he went on. "They cut a deal. You wanna try something? Their pale ale is good. Or is that not allowed? I heard you had a new boss there—another crazy Beaumont. Two of them, even!" He chuckled and shook his head in disbelief. "You think the Beaumonts knew their brother or half brother or whatever he is took over? I heard it might have been planned…"

It took everything Casey had not to look back over her shoulder at Zeb. Maybe she was reading too much into the situation, but she would put money on the fact that he wasn't grinning anymore. "I bet it was a hell of a surprise," she said, desperate to change the subject. "Give me the pale ale and—"

"Nachos, extra jalapeños?" He winked at her. "I'm on it."

"A *hell* of a surprise," Zeb whispered in her ear. The closeness of his voice was so unexpected that she jumped. But just then Marco came back with her order.

"Gotta say," Marco went on, ringing up her total, "it was good to see a brother up there, though. I mean…he was black, right?"

Behind her, Zeb made a noise that sounded like it was somewhere between a laugh and a choke. "It doesn't really matter," she said honestly as she handed over the cash, "as long as we get the beer right."

"Ah, that's what I like about you, Casey—a woman who knows her beer." He gave her a moony look, as if he were dazzled by beauty they both knew she didn't have. "It's not too late to marry me, you know that?"

Hand to God, Casey thought she heard Zeb growl behind her.

Okay, that was not the kind of noise a boss made when an employee engaged in chitchat with a— Well, Marco sold beer. So with a colleague of sorts. However, it was the sort of noise a man on a date made.

Not a date. *Not* a date.

For the first time, Marco seemed to notice the looming Braves fan behind her. "Come back and see me at the fifth?" Marco pleaded, keeping a cautious eye on Zeb.

"You know I will. And have Kenny bring me a stout in the third, okay?" She and Dad didn't have the super-expensive seats where people took her order and delivered it to her. But Kenny the beer vendor would bring them another beer in the third and again in the seventh—and not the beer he hawked to everyone else.

She got her nachos and her beer and moved off to the side. It was then she noticed that Zeb's eyes hadn't left her.

A shiver of heat went through her because Zeb's gaze was intense. He looked at her like…like she didn't even know what. She wasn't sure she wanted to find out, because what if he could see right through her?

What if he could see how much she was attracted to *him*?

This was a bad idea. She was on a date with her brand-new CEO and he was hot and funny and brooding all at once and they were drinking their chief competitor's product and…

Zeb glanced over at her as he paid for his food and shot another warm grin at her.

And she was in trouble. Big, *big* trouble.

# Seven

Zeb followed Casey to the seats. He tried his best to keep his gaze locked on the swinging ponytail that hung out the back of her Rockies hat—and not on her backside.

That was proving to be quite a challenge, though, because her backside was a sight to behold. Her jeans clung to her curves in all the right ways. Why hadn't he noticed that before?

Oh, yeah—the lab coat.

Which hadn't shown him the real woman. But this? A bright young woman with hips and curves who was friends with everyone and completely at home in the male bastion of a baseball stadium?

Who'd said—out loud—that it didn't matter if Zeb was black or not?

She turned suddenly and he snapped his gaze back up to her face. "Here," she said, notching an eyebrow at him and gesturing toward a nearly empty row. "Seats nine and ten."

They were eight rows off the first baseline, right behind the dugout. "Great seats," he told her. "I didn't bring my glove."

She snorted as she worked her way down the row. "Definitely keep your eyes on the ball here. You never know."

He made his way to seat nine. There weren't many people around, but he had a feeling that if there had been, they'd all have known Casey.

"What did you get?" she asked once they were seated.

"The Percheron lager."

"Oh, that's such a nice beer," she said with a wistful sigh.

"Yeah?" He held out his plastic collector's cup to her. "Have a drink."

She looked at him for a long moment and then leaned over and pressed her lips against the rim of his cup. Fascinated, he watched as her mouth opened and she took a sip.

Heat shot through his body, driving his pulse to a sudden pounding in his veins. It only got worse when she leaned back just enough that she could sweep her tongue over her lips, getting every last drop of beer.

*Damn.* Watching Casey Johnson drink beer was almost a holy experience.

*Greedy* was not a word he embraced. *Greedy* implied a lack of control—stupid mistakes and rash consequences. He was not a greedy person. He was methodical and detailed and careful. Always.

But right now he wanted. He wanted her lips to drink him in like she'd drunk the beer. He wanted her tongue to sweep over his lips with that slow intensity. God help him, he wanted her to savor him. And if that made him greedy, then so be it.

So, carefully, he turned the cup around and put his lips where hers had been. Her eyes darkened as he drank. "You're right," he said, the taste of the beer and of Casey mixing on his tongue. "It's a beautiful beer."

Her breath caught and her cheeks colored, throwing the spiderweb scar on her cheek into high relief. And then, heaven help him, she leaned toward him. She could have leaned away, turned away—done something to put distance between them. She could have made it clear that she didn't want him at all.

But she didn't. She felt it, too, this connection between them. Her lips parted ever so slightly and she leaned forward, close enough for him to touch. Close enough for him to take a sip.

The crack of a bat and the crowd cheering snapped his attention away. His head was buzzing as if he'd chugged a six-pack.

"Did they score?" Casey asked, shaking off her

confusion. Then she did lean away, settling back into her chair.

Zeb immediately tamped down that rush of lust. They were in public, for God's sake. This wasn't like him. He didn't go for women like Casey—she was the walking embodiment of a tomboy. Women he favored were cultured and refined, elegant and beautiful. They were everything he'd spent his life trying to become.

Accepted. Welcomed. They belonged in the finest social circles.

Women he liked would never sit on the first-base side and hope to catch a fly ball. They wouldn't appreciate the finer points of an IPA or a lager. They wouldn't be proud of a father who was an electrician and they wouldn't be caught dead in a baseball hat—but Casey?

She was rough-and-tumble and there was a decent chance she could best him in an arm-wrestling contest. There shouldn't have been a single thing about her that he found attractive.

So why couldn't he stop staring at her?

Because he couldn't. "Did you want to try mine? I helped develop it."

He leaned close to her and waited until she held the cup up to his lips. He couldn't tear his gaze away from hers, though. He saw when she sucked in a gasp when he ran his tongue over the rim before he reached up and placed his palm on the bottom of the cup, slowly tilting it back. The bitterness of the brew washed over him.

It wasn't like he'd never had an IPA before. But this was different. He could taste the beer, sure. But there was something about the brightness of the hops, the way it danced on his tongue—it tasted like…

Like her.

"It's really good," he told her. "You developed it?"

"I did. Percheron was, um…"

"It's all right," he said, leaning back. "I don't think if you say Chadwick's name three times, he magically appears. I understand the company's history."

"Oh. Okay." Damn, that blush only made her look prettier. "Well, Percheron was Chadwick's pet project and I'd been there for almost ten years by that point and he let me help. I was the assistant brewmaster for Percheron when he…" Her voice trailed off and she turned to face the field. "When he left."

Zeb mulled that over a bit. "Why didn't you go with him?"

"Because the brewmaster did and Chadwick wanted to actually make the beer himself. Percheron is a much smaller company."

He heard the sorrow in her voice. She'd wanted to go with her old boss—that much was clear.

Then she turned a wide smile in his direction. "Plus, if I'd left the brewery, I'd still be an assistant brewmaster. I'm the brewmaster for the third-largest brewery in the country because I outlasted everyone else. Attrition isn't the best way to get a promotion but it was effective nonetheless."

"That's what you wanted?"

She looked smug, the cat that had all the cream to herself. His pulse picked up another notch. "That's what I wanted."

Underneath that beer-drinking, sports-loving exterior, Zeb had to admire the sheer ambition of this woman. Not just anyone would set out to be the first—or youngest—female brewmaster in the country.

But Casey would. And she'd accomplished her goal.

Zeb took a long drink of his lager. It was good, too. "So, Percheron Drafts was your baby?"

"It was Chadwick's, but I was Igor to his Frankenstein."

He laughed—a deep, long sound that shocked him. That kind of laugh wasn't dignified or intimidating. Zeb didn't allow himself to laugh like that, because he was a CEO and he had to instill fear in the hearts of his enemies.

Except...except he was at a ball game, kicking back with a pretty girl and a beer, and his team was at the plate and the weather was warm and it was...

...perfect.

"So I want you to make Percheron—or something like it—your baby again."

Even though he wasn't looking at Casey, he felt the current of tension pass through her. "What?"

"I understand Chadwick started Percheron Drafts to compete with the explosion of craft breweries. And we lost that. I don't want to throw in that particular towel just yet. So, you want to try experimental beers? That's what I want you to do, too."

She turned to face him again, and dammit, she practically glowed. Maybe it was just the setting sun, but he didn't think so. She looked so happy—and he'd put that look on her face.

"Thank you," she said in a voice so quiet that he had to lean forward to hear it. "When you started, I thought..."

He smirked. She'd thought many things, he'd be willing to bet—and precious few of them had been good.

"Can you keep a secret?" he asked.

Her lips twisted in what he hoped was an amused grin. "How many times are you going to ask me that?"

"I'm not such a bad guy," he went on, ignoring her sass. "But don't tell anyone."

She mimed locking her lips and throwing the key over her shoulder.

Somewhere in the background, a ball game was happening. And he loved sports, he really did. But he had questions. He'd learned a little more about what kind of man his half brother was but that was just the tip of the iceberg.

But the spell of the moment had been broken. They settled in and watched the game. Sure enough, by the third inning, a grizzled older man came around with a stout for Casey. Zeb didn't warrant that level of personal service—certainly not in the opposing team's colors. As he sipped the flagship beer of his second-largest competitor, he decided it was…serviceable. Just as Casey had described their own beer.

A fact that was only highlighted when Casey let him sip her stout. "It's going to be tough to beat," he said with a sigh as she took a long drink.

For the first time, he had a doubt about what he was doing. He'd spent years—*years*—plotting and scheming to get his birthright back. He was a Beaumont and he was going to make sure everyone knew it.

But now, sitting here and drinking his half brother's beer…

He was reminded once again what he didn't have. Chadwick had literally decades to learn about the business of the brewery and the craft of beer. And Zeb—well, he knew a hell of a lot about business. But he hadn't learned it at his father's knee. Beer was his birthright—but he couldn't whip up his own batch if his life depended on it.

Casey patted his arm. "We don't have to beat it." She paused and he heard her clear her throat. "Unless…"

"Unless what?"

She looked into her cup. It was half-empty. "Unless you're out to destroy Percheron Drafts."

That was what she said. What she was really asking was, *Are you out to destroy the other Beaumonts?* It was a fair question.

"Because that's kind of a big thing," she went on in a quiet voice, looking anywhere but at him. "I don't know how many people would be supportive of that. At work, I mean." She grimaced. "There might be a lot of resignations."

She wouldn't be supportive of that. She would quit. She'd quit and go elsewhere because even though her first loyalty was to herself and then the beer, the Beaumont family was pretty high on her list.

Again, he wondered how she'd come to this point in her life. The youngest female brewmaster at the third-largest brewery in the country. He might not know the details of her story, but he recognized this one simple truth: she was who she was in large part because the Beaumonts had given her a chance. Because she'd been Igor to Chadwick Beaumont's Frankenstein.

She'd give up her dream job if it came down to a choice between the Beaumont Brewery and Percheron Drafts.

This thought made him more than a little uncomfortable because he could try to explain how it was all business, how this was a battle for market share between two corporations and corporations were not people, but none of that was entirely true.

If he forced her to choose between the Beaumonts and himself, she'd choose them over him.

"There was a time," he said in a quiet voice, "when I wanted to destroy them."

Her head snapped up. "What?"

"I used to hate them. They had everything and I had nothing." Nothing but a bitter mother and a head for business.

"But…" She stared at him, her mouth open wide. "But *look* at you. You're rich and powerful and hot and you did that all on your own." He blinked at her, but she didn't seem to be aware of what she'd just said, because she went on without missing a beat, "Some of those Beaumonts— I mean, don't get me wrong—I like them. But they're more than a little messed up. Trust me. I was around them long enough to see how the public image wasn't reality. Phillip was a hot mess and Chadwick was miserable and Frances… I mean, they had everything handed to them and it didn't make them any happier." She shook her head and slouched back in her seat.

And suddenly, he felt he had to make her understand that this wasn't about his siblings, because he was an adult and he realized now what he hadn't known as a child—that his siblings were younger than he was and probably knew only what the rest of the world did about Hardwick Beaumont.

"Casey," he said. She looked at him and he could see how nervous she was. "I was going to say that I used to hate them—but I don't. How could I? I don't know them and I doubt any of them knew a thing about me before that press conference. I'm not out to destroy them and I'm not out to destroy Percheron Drafts. It's enough that I have the brewery."

She looked at him then—really looked at him. Zeb started to squirm in his seat, because, honestly? He didn't know what she saw. Did she see a man who made sure his mom had a booming business and his best friend had a good-paying job he loved? Did she see a son who'd never know his father?

Or—worse—would she see a boy rejected by his family, a man who wasn't black and wasn't white but who occupied a no-man's-land in the middle? Would she see an impostor who'd decided he was a Beaumont, regardless of how true it might actually be?

He didn't want to know what she saw. Because quite unexpectedly, Casey Johnson's opinion had become important to him and he didn't want to know if she didn't approve of him.

So he quickly changed the subject. "Tell me…" he said, keeping his voice casual as he turned his attention back to the field. He didn't even know what inning it was anymore. There—the scoreboard said fourth. The home team was at the plate and they already had two outs. Almost halfway done with this corporate outing. "Does that happen often?"

"What? Your boss admitting that he's not a total bastard?"

Zeb choked on his beer. "Actually, I meant that guy proposing to you."

"Who, Marco?" She snorted. "He proposes every time I see him. And since I have season tickets…"

"What does your dad think of that?"

That got him a serious side-eye. "First off, Marco's joking. Second off, my father is many things, but he's not my keeper. And third off—why do you care?"

"I don't," he answered quickly. Maybe too quickly. "Just trying to get a fuller picture of the one person responsible for keeping my company afloat."

She snorted as a pop fly ended the inning. "Come on," she said, standing and stretching. "Let's go."

Slowly, they worked their way out of the seats and back to the concession stands. He got a stout for himself and Casey got a porter. Marco flirted shamelessly but this time, Zeb focused on Casey. She smiled and joked, but at no point did she look at the young man the way she'd looked at him earlier. She didn't blush and she didn't lean toward Marco.

There was no heat. She was exactly as she appeared—a friendly tomboy. The difference between this woman and the one who'd blushed so prettily back in the seats, whose eyes had dilated and who'd leaned toward him with desire writ large on her face—that difference was huge.

With more beer and more nachos, they made their way back to their seats. As odd as it was, Zeb was having trouble remembering the last time he'd taken a night off like this. Yeah, they were still talking beer and competitors but…

But he was having fun. He was three beers in and

even though he wasn't drunk—not even close—he was more relaxed than he'd been in a long time. It'd been months of watching and waiting to make sure all the final pieces of the puzzle were in place, and he was pretty sure he hadn't stopped to appreciate all that he'd accomplished.

Well, sort of relaxed. There was something else the beer vendor—Marco—had said that itched at the back of Zeb's mind.

"Did you mean what you said?" he blurted out. Hmm. Maybe he was a little more buzzed than he thought.

There was a longish pause before she said, "About?"

"That it didn't matter if I was black or not." Because it always mattered. *Always.* He was either "exotic" because he had an African American mother and green eyes or he was black and a borderline thug. He never got to be just a businessman. He was always a black businessman.

It was something white people never even thought about. But he always had that extra hurdle to clear. He didn't get to make mistakes, because even one would be proof that he couldn't cut it.

Not that he was complaining. He'd learned his lesson early in life—no one was going to give him a single damned thing. Not his father, not his family, not the world. Everything he wanted out of this life, he had to take. Being a black businessman made him a tougher negotiator, a sharper investor.

He wanted the brewery and the legitimacy that

came with it. He wanted his father's approval and, short of that, he wanted the extended Beaumont family to know who he was.

He was Zebadiah Richards and he would not be ignored.

Not that Casey was ignoring him. She'd turned to look at him again—and for the second time tonight, he thought she was seeing more than he wanted her to.

Dammit, he should have kept his mouth shut.

"You tell me—does it matter?"

"It shouldn't." More than anything, he wanted it to not matter.

She shrugged. "Then it doesn't."

He should let this go. He had his victory—of sorts—and besides, what did it matter if she looked at him and saw a black CEO or just a CEO?

*Or even*, a small voice in the back of his mind whispered, *something other than a CEO? Something more?*

But he couldn't revel in his small victory. He needed to know—was she serious or was she paying lip service because he was her boss? "So you're saying it doesn't matter that my mother spent the last thirty-seven years doing hair in a black neighborhood in Atlanta? That I went to a historically black college? That people have pulled out of deals with me because no matter how light skinned I am, I'll never be white enough?"

He hadn't meant to say all of that. But the only

thing worse than his skin color being the first—and sometimes only—thing people used to define him was when people tried to explain they didn't "see color." They meant well—he knew that—but the truth was, it *did* matter. He'd made his first fortune for his mother, merchandising a line of weave and braid products for upper-class African American consumers that had, thanks to millennials, reached a small level of crossover success in the mainstream market. When people said they didn't see color, they effectively erased the blackness from his life.

Being African American wasn't who he was—but it was a part of him. And for some reason, he needed her to understand that.

He had her full attention now. Her gaze swept over him and he felt his muscles tighten, almost as if he were in fight-or-flight mode. And he didn't run. He never ran.

"Will our beer suddenly taste black?" she asked.

"Don't be ridiculous. We might broaden our marketing reach, though."

She tilted her head. "All I care about is the beer."

"Seriously?"

She sighed heavily. "Let me ask you this—when you drink a Rocky Top beer, does it taste feminine?"

"You're being ridiculous."

That got him a hard glare. A glare he probably deserved, but still. "Zeb, I don't know what you want me to say here. Of course it matters, because that's your life. That's who you are. But I can't hold that against you, and anyway, why would I want to? You didn't ask for that. You can't change that, any more than I can change the fact that my mother died in a car accident when I was two and left me with this," she said, pointing to her scarred cheek, "and my father raised me as best he could—and that meant beer and sports and changing my own oil in my car. We both exist in a space that someone else is always going to say we shouldn't—so what? We're here. We like beer." She grinned hugely at him. "Get used to it."

Everything around him went still. He wasn't breathing. He wasn't sure his heart was even beating. He didn't hear the sounds of the game or the chatter of the fans around them.

His entire world narrowed to her. All he could see and hear and feel—because dammit, she was close enough that their forearms kept touching, their knees bumping—was Casey.

It mattered. *He* mattered. No conditions, no exceptions. He mattered just the way he was.

Had anyone ever said as much to him? Even his own mother? No. What had mattered was what he wasn't. He wasn't a Beaumont. He wasn't legitimate. He wasn't white.

Something in his chest unclenched, something he'd never known he was holding tightly. Something that felt like…

…peace.

He dimly heard a loud crack and then Casey jolted and shouted, "Look out!"

Zeb moved without thinking. He was in a weird space—everything happened as if it were in slow motion. His head turned like he was stuck in molasses, like the baseball was coming directly for him at a snail's pace. He reached out slowly and caught the fly ball a few inches from Casey's shoulder.

The pain of the ball smacking into his palm snapped him out of it. "Damn," he hissed, shaking his hand as a smattering of applause broke out from the crowd. "That hurt."

Casey turned her face toward him, her eyes wide. There was an unfamiliar feeling trying to make its way to the forefront of Zeb's mind as he stared into her beautiful light brown eyes, one he couldn't name. He wasn't sure he wanted to.

"You caught the ball bare-handed," she said, her voice breathy. Then, before Zeb could do anything, she looked down to where he was still holding the foul ball. She moved slowly when she pulled the ball out of his palm and stared at his reddening skin. Lightly, so lightly it almost hurt, she traced her fingertip over the palm of his hand. "Did it hurt?"

That unnamed, unfamiliar feeling was immediately buried under something that was much easier to identify—lust. "Not much," he said, and he didn't miss the way his voice dropped. He had a vague sense that he wasn't being entirely honest—it hurt enough to snap him out of his reverie. But with her stroking his skin…

…everything felt just fine.

And it got a whole lot better when she lifted his hand and pressed a kiss against his palm. "Do we need to go and get some ice or…?"

*Or*? *Or* sounded good. *Or* sounded great. "Only if you want to," he told her, shifting so that he was cupping her cheek in his hand. "Your call."

Because he wasn't talking about ice. Or beer. Or baseball.

He dragged his thumb over the top of her cheek as she leaned into his touch. She lifted her gaze to his face and for a second, he thought he'd taken it too far. He'd misread the signals and she would storm out of the stadium just like she'd stormed out of his office that first day. She would quit and he would deserve it.

Except she didn't. "I live a block away," she said, and he heard the slightest shiver in her voice, felt a matching shiver in her body. "If that's what you need."

What did he need? It should've been a simple question with a simple answer—her. Right now he needed her.

But there was nothing simple about Casey Johnson and everything got much more complicated when she pressed his hand closer to her cheek.

For the first time in a very long time, Zeb was at a loss for words. It wasn't like him. When it came to women, he'd always known what to say, when to say it. Growing up in a hair salon had given him plenty of opportunity to learn what women wanted, what they needed and where those two things met and when they didn't. *Smooth*, more than one of his paramours had called him. And he was. Smooth and cool and…cold. Distant. Reserved.

He didn't feel any of those things right now. All he could feel was the heat that flowed between her skin and his.

"I need to cool down," he told her, only dimly aware that that was not the smoothest line he had ever uttered. But he didn't have anything else right now. His hand was throbbing and his blood was throbbing and his dick—that, especially, was throbbing. Everything about him was hot and hard, and even though he was no innocent wallflower, it all felt strange and new. He felt strange and new because Casey saw him in a way that no one else did.

He didn't know what was going to happen. Even if all she did was take him back to her place and stick some ice on his hand, that was fine, too. He was not going to be *that* guy.

Still, when she said, "Come with me," Zeb hoped that he could do exactly that.

# Eight

Was she seriously doing this? Taking Zeb Richards back to her apartment?

Well, obviously, she was. She was holding his not-wounded hand and leading him away from the stadium. So there really wasn't any question about what was happening here.

This was crazy. Absolutely crazy. She shouldn't be taking him back to her apartment, she shouldn't be holding his hand and she most especially shouldn't be thinking about what would happen when they got there.

But she was. She was thinking about peeling that T-shirt off him and running her hands over his muscles and…

His fingers tightened around hers and he pulled her a step closer to him. He was hot in a way that she hadn't anticipated. Heat radiated off his body, so much so that she thought the edges around his skin might waver like a mirage if she looked at him head-on.

She swallowed and tried to think of things she had done that were crazier than this. Walking into the brewery and demanding a job—that had been pretty bold. And there was that summer fling with a rookie on the Rockies—but he'd been traded to Seattle in the off-season and their paths didn't cross anymore. That had been wild and a hell of a lot of fun.

But nothing came close to bringing the new CEO of the Beaumont Brewery home with her. And the thing was, she wasn't entirely sure what had changed. One moment, they'd been talking—okay, flirting. They'd been flirting. But it seemed…innocent, almost.

And then she had told him about her mom dying in a car accident and he caught that ball before it hit her—she still didn't know how the hell he'd managed that—and everything had changed.

And now she was bringing her boss home with her.

Except that wasn't true, either. It was—but it also wasn't. She wasn't bringing home the ice-cold man in a suit who'd had the sheer nerve to call a press conference and announce that he was one of the Beaumont bastards. That man was fascinating—but that wasn't who was holding her hand.

She was bringing Zeb home. The son of a hairdresser who liked baseball and didn't look at her like she was his best friend or, worse, one of the guys.

She was probably going to regret this. But she didn't care right now. Because Zeb was looking at her and she felt beautiful, sensual, desirable and so very feminine. And that was what she wanted, even if it was for only a little while.

They made it back to her apartment. She led him to the elevator. Even standing here, holding his hand, felt off. This was the part she was never any good at. Sitting in front of the game with beers in their hands—yes. Then she could talk and flirt and be herself. But when she wanted to be that beautiful, desirable creature men craved…she froze up. It was not a pleasant sensation.

The elevator doors opened and they stepped inside. Casey hit the button for the fifth floor and the door slid shut. The next thing she knew, Zeb had pressed into the back of the elevator. His body held hers against the wall—but other than that, he didn't touch her and he didn't kiss her.

"Tell me I didn't read you wrong back there," he said, his voice low and husky. It sent a shiver down her spine and one corner of his mouth curved up into a cocky half smile. He lifted one hand and moved as if he were going to touch her face—but didn't. "Casey…"

This was her out—if she wanted it. She could laugh it off and say, *Gosh, how's your hand?* And that'd be that.

"You didn't," she whispered.

Then he did touch her. He cupped her cheek in his hand and tilted her head up. "Do I really matter to you?" he whispered against her skin. "Or are you just here for the beer?"

If Casey allowed herself to admit that she had thought of this moment before right now—and she wasn't necessarily admitting to anything—she hadn't pictured this. She assumed Zeb would pin her against the wall or his desk and seduce her ruthlessly. Not that there was anything wrong with being seduced ruthlessly—it had its place in the world and her fantasies.

But this tenderness? She didn't quite know what to make of it.

"At work tomorrow," she said, squinting her eyes shut because the last thing she wanted to think about was the number of company policies she was about to break, "it's about the beer." She felt Zeb tense and then there was a little bit of space between their bodies as he stepped away from her.

Oh, no. She wasn't going to let him go. Not when she had him right where she wanted him. She locked her arms around his neck and pulled him back into her. "But we're not at work right now, are we?"

"Right," he agreed. Her body molded to his and his to hers. "Nothing at work. But outside of work…"

Then he kissed her. And that? *That* bordered on a ruthless seduction because it wasn't a gentle, tentative touch of two lips meeting and exploring for the first time. No, when he kissed her, he *claimed* her. The heat from his mouth seared her, and suddenly, she was too hot—for the elevator, for her clothes, for any of it.

"Tell me what you want," he said again when his lips trailed over her jaw and down her neck.

This was crazy—but the very best kind of crazy. Carte blanche with someone as strong and hot and masculine as Zeb Richards? Oh, yeah, this was the stuff of fantasies.

She started to say what she always said. "Tell me—"

Just then, the elevator came to a stop and the door opened. Damn. She'd forgotten they weren't actually in her apartment yet.

Zeb pushed back as she fumbled around for her keys. Hopefully, that would be the last interruption for at least the next hour. Quickly, she led him down the hall. "It's not much," she explained, suddenly nervous all over again. Her studio apartment was certainly not one of the grand old mansions of Denver.

She unlocked the door. Zeb followed her in, and once the door was shut behind them, he put his hands on her hips. "Nice place," he said, and she could tell from the tone of his voice that he wasn't looking at her apartment at all. "Beautiful views," he added, and then he was pulling the hem of her shirt, lifting it until he accidentally knocked her hat off her head. The whole thing got hung up on her ponytail and, laughing, she reached around to help untangle it.

"What would you like me to tell you?" As he spoke, his lips were against the base of her neck, his teeth skimming over her sensitive skin.

She couldn't stop the shiver that went through her. "Tell me…" She opened her mouth to explain that she wanted to feel pretty—but stopped because she couldn't figure out how to say it without sounding lame, desperate even. And besides, wanting to feel pretty—it didn't exactly mesh with her fantasy about a ruthless seduction. So she hedged. She always hedged. "…what you're going to do to me."

In the past, that had worked like a charm. Ask for a little dirty talk? The cocky young men she brought home were always ready and willing.

But Zeb wasn't. Instead, he stood behind her, skimming the tips of his fingers over her shoulders and down her bare back. He didn't even wrench her bra off her, for crying out loud. All he did was… touch her.

Not that she was complaining about being touched. Her eyelids fluttered shut and she leaned into his touch.

"You still haven't told me what you want. I'm more than happy to describe it for you, but I need to know what I should be doing in the first place. For instance…" One hand removed itself from her skin. The next thing she knew, he wrapped her ponytail around his hand and pivoted, bringing her against the small countertop in her kitchen. "I could bend you over and take you hard and fast right here." He pulled her hair just enough that she had to lean back. "And I'd make sure you screamed when you came," he growled as he slipped his hand down over the seam of her jeans. With exquisite precision, he pressed against her most sensitive spot.

*"Oh,"* she gasped, writhing against his hand. Her pulse pounded against where he was touching her and he used her ponytail to tilt her head so he could do more than skim his teeth over her neck. He bit down and, with the smallest movement of his hand, almost brought her to her knees. *"Zeb."*

And then the bastard stopped. "But maybe you don't like it rough," he said in the most casual voice she'd ever heard as he pulled his hands away from her ponytail and her pants. What the hell?

Then his hands were tracing the lines of her shoulders again.

"Maybe you want slow, sensual seduction, where I start kissing here…" he murmured against her neck. Then his lips moved down over her shoulder and he slid his hands up her waist to cup her breasts. "And there."

This time, both hands slid over the front of her jeans and maybe it was shameless, but she arched her back and opened for him. "And everywhere," he finished. "Until you can't take it."

And then he stopped *again*.

What was happening here? Because in the past, when she told someone to talk dirty to her, it got crude *fast*. And it wasn't like the sex was bad—it was good. She liked it. But it felt like…

It always felt like that was the best she could hope for. She wasn't pretty and she wasn't soft and she wasn't feminine, and so crude, fast sex was the best she could expect any man to do when faced with her naked.

And suddenly, she realized that wasn't what she wanted. Not anymore. Not from him.

"Maybe you want to be in charge," he went on, his voice so deep but different, too, because now there was that trace of a Southern accent coming through. It sounded like sin on the wind, that voice—honey sweet with just a hint of danger to it. He spun her around so he was leaning back on the counter and she had him boxed in. He dropped his hands and stared at her hungrily with those beautiful eyes. "Maybe I need to step back and let you show me what you want."

It was an intense feeling, being in Zeb Richards's sights.

"So what's it going to be?" But even as he asked it—sounding cool and calm and in complete control—she saw a muscle in his jaw tic and a tremor pass through his body. His gaze dipped down to her breasts, to her lucky purple bra that she wore to every home game, and a growl that she felt in her very center came rumbling out of his chest. He was hanging on to his control by the very thinnest of threads. Because of her.

He was waiting, she realized. It was her move. So that was what she did. She reached up and pulled his hat off his head and launched it somewhere in the middle of her apartment. He leaned toward her but he didn't touch her.

"What about you? What do you want?" she asked.

He shook his head in mock disappointment even as he smiled slyly at her. "I have this rule—if you don't tell me what you want, I won't give it to you. No mixed signals, no mind reading. I'm not going to guess and risk being wrong."

This wasn't working, she decided. At the very least, it wasn't what she was used to. All this... talking. It wasn't what she was good at. It only highlighted how awkward she was at things like seduction and romance, things that came naturally to other women.

She appreciated the fact that he wanted to be sure about her, about this—really, she did. But she didn't want to think. She didn't want each interaction to be a negotiation. She wanted to be swept away so she could pretend, if only for a little while, that she was soft and sultry and beautiful.

And she'd never get to hold on to that fantasy if she had to explain what she wanted, because explaining would only draw attention to what she wasn't.

Which left only one possible conclusion, really. She was done talking.

She leaned forward and grabbed the hem of his shirt. In one swift motion, she pulled it up and over his head and tossed it on the floor. And right about then, she not only stopped talking but stopped thinking.

Because Zeb's chest was a sight to behold. That T-shirt hadn't been lying. *Muscles*, she thought dimly as she reached out to stroke her hand over one of his packs. So many muscles.

"Casey…" He almost moaned when she skimmed her hand over his bare skin and moved lower. As she palmed the rippling muscles of his abs, he sucked in a breath and gripped the countertop so hard she could see his arms shaking. "You're killing me, woman."

That was better, she decided. She couldn't pull off seductive, but there was a lot to be said for raw sexual energy. That, at least, she could handle.

So she decided to handle it. Personally. She hooked her hands into the waistband of his jeans and pulled his hips toward her. As she did so, she started working at the buttons of his fly. His chest promised great, great things and she wanted to see if the rest of him could deliver on that promise.

"What do you want to hear?" he asked in that low, sensual voice that was summer sex on the wind.

*Tell me I'm pretty.*

But she couldn't say that, because she knew what would happen. She would ask him to tell her she was pretty and he would. He would probably even make it sound so good that she would believe him. After all, she thought as she pushed his jeans down and cupped him through his boxer briefs, what guy wouldn't find a woman who was about to sleep with him pretty?

She'd been here before, too. She might be pretty enough in the heat of the moment but the second the climactic high began to fade, so did any perceived beauty she possessed. Then she'd get her decidedly unfeminine clothes back on and before she knew it, she'd be one of the boys again.

She didn't just want him to tell her she was pretty or beautiful or sensual or any of those things. She wanted him to make her believe it, all of it, today, tomorrow and into next week, at the very least. And *that* was a trick no one had been able to master yet.

So she gave the waistband of his briefs a tug and freed him. He sprang to attention as a low groan issued from Zeb's throat.

Immediately, her jaw dropped. "Oh, Zeb," she breathed as she wrapped one and then the other hand around his girth, one on top of the other. Slowly, she stroked up the length of him and then back down. Then she looked up at him and caught him watching her. "I am *impressed*."

He thrust in her hands—but even that was controlled. They were standing in her kitchen, both shirtless, and she was stroking him—and he wasn't even touching her. Sure, the look in his eyes was enough to make her shiver with want because she was having an impact. The cords of his neck tightened and his jaw clenched as his length slid in her grip.

But it wasn't enough. She needed more. "Feel free to join in," she told him.

"You're doing a pretty damn good job all by yourself," he ground out through gritted teeth. But even as he said it, he pried one hand off the countertop and gripped the back of her neck, pulling her into his chest. God, he was almost red-hot to the touch and all she wanted to do was be burned.

"Stop holding back." It came out as an order, but what was she supposed to do? If he was holding back out of some sort of sense of chivalry—however misguided—or consent or whatever, then she needed to get that cleared up right now.

She needed to tell him what she wanted—he'd already told her she had to, right? But she couldn't figure out how to say it without sounding sad about it, so instead, she fell back on the tried-and-true. "You've got what I want," she said as she gave him a firm squeeze. "So show me what you can do with it."

There was just a moment's hesitation—the calm before the storm, she realized. Zeb's eyes darkened and his fingers flexed against the back of her neck.

And then he exploded into movement. Casey was spun around and lifted up onto the countertop, her legs parted as he stepped into her. It happened so fast that she was almost dizzy. And *that* was what she needed right now. She needed his lips on her mouth, her neck, her chest. She needed his fingertips smoothly unhooking her lucky bra and she needed to hear the groan of desire when the bra fell to the ground.

"Damn, Casey—look at you," he said in a tone that was almost reverential.

Casey's eyes drifted shut as he stroked his fingertips over the tops of her breasts and then around her nipples.

"Yes," she whispered as he leaned down to take her in his mouth. His teeth scraped over her sensitive skin and then he sucked on her. "Oh, yes," she hissed, holding him to her.

His hand slid around her back and pulled her to the edge of the counter and then he was grinding against her, his erection hard and hot and everything she wanted—well, almost everything. There was the unfortunate matter of her jeans and the barrier they formed between the two of them.

"This is what you want, isn't it?" Zeb thrust against her. "You want me to take you here, on the countertop, because I can't wait long enough to get you into a bed?"

Every word was punctuated by another thrust. And every thrust was punctuated by a low moan that Casey couldn't have held if she'd tried.

"God, yes," she whimpered as her hips shimmied against his. This was better. Zeb was overpowering her senses, hard and fast. She didn't want to think. She just wanted to feel.

"I wonder," he said in a voice that bordered on ruthless, "if I should bite you here," he said as he traced a pattern on her shoulders with his tongue, "or here—" and he kissed the top of her left breast "—or…here." With that, he crouched down and nipped her inner thigh, and even though she could barely feel his teeth through the denim, she still shuddered with anticipation. This was better. This was things going according to script.

"D, all of the above." It was at that point that she discovered a problem. Zeb wore his hair close-cropped—there was nothing for her to thread her fingers through, nothing for her to hold on to as he rubbed along the seam of her jeans, over her very center.

But her hips bucked when he pressed against her. "Look at you," he growled as he came to his feet. "Just look at you."

She sucked in a ragged gasp when his hands moved and then he was undoing the button of her jeans and sliding down the zipper.

"I'd rather look at you," she told him as she lifted one hip and then the other off the countertop so he could work her jeans down. "You are, hands down, the most gorgeous man I've ever seen."

She let her hands skim over his shoulders and down his arms. It wasn't fair—there wasn't an ounce of fat on him. She was going to have to revise her opinion of men in suits, she thought dimly as he peeled her jeans the rest of the way off her legs.

"I can't wait," he growled in her ear, the raw urgency in his voice sending another shiver of desire through her body. He pulled the thin cotton of her panties to one side and then his erection was grinding directly against her. "Are you on something? Do you have something?"

"I'm on the Pill," she told him, her hips flexing to meet his. In that moment, she did feel desirable and wanted. His finger tested her body and she moaned into him. She might not be sensual or gorgeous, but she could still do this to a man—drive him so crazy with need that he couldn't even wait to get her undressed all the way.

"Now," she told him. "Now, Zeb. Please."

She didn't have to ask twice. He positioned himself at her entrance. "You're so ready for me. God, just look at you." But he didn't thrust into her. Instead, it appeared he was actually going to look at her.

She pushed back against her insecurity as he studied her. She knew she couldn't measure up to his other lovers—a man that looked like him? He could have his pick of women. Hell, she wasn't even sure why he was here with her—except for the fact that she was…well, *available*. "Why are you stopping? Don't stop."

"Is that how you want it? Hard and fast?" Even as he asked, he moved, pushing into her inch by agonizing inch.

"Zeb." Even as she wrapped her legs around his hips and tried to draw him in farther. And when that worked only to a point, she wrapped her arms around his waist and dug her fingernails into his back.

That did the trick. With a roar of desire, he thrust forward and sank all the way into her. Oh, *God.* She took him in easily, moaning with desire. "Is that what you want?"

She heard his self-control hanging by a thread.

So she raked her nails up and down his back— not hard enough to break skin, but more than enough that he could feel it. He withdrew and thrust into her again, this time harder and faster.

"Yes," she whimpered. "More." She leaned her head back, lifting her chest up to him. "I need more."

Without breaking rhythm, he bent down and nipped at her breast again.

"More," she demanded because she was already so, so close. She needed just a little something to push her over the edge.

"I love a woman who knows what she wants." He sucked her nipple into his mouth—hard. There was just a hint of pain around the edges of the pleasure and it shocked her to her very core in the best way possible.

"Oh, God—" But anything else she would've tried to say got lost as his mouth worked on her and he buried himself in her again and again.

The orgasm snapped back on her like a rubber band pulled too tight, so strong she couldn't even cry out. She couldn't breathe—she couldn't think. All she could do was feel. It was everything she wanted and more. Everything she'd wanted since she'd stormed into his office that very first day and seen him. Ruthless seduction and mind-blowing climaxes and want and need all blended together into mindless pleasure.

Zeb relinquished his hold on her breast and buried his face in her neck, driving in harder and harder. She felt his teeth on her again, just as he promised. And then his hands moved between them and his thumb pressed against her sex as he thrust harder, and this time, Casey did scream. The orgasm shook through her and left her rag-doll limp as he thrust one final time and then froze. His shoulders slumped and he pulled her in close.

"God, Casey…" She took it as a source of personal pride that he sounded shaky. "That was *amazing*."

All she could do was sigh. That was enough. She'd take *amazing* every day of the week.

And then he had to go and ruin it.

He leaned back and shot her a surprised smile and said, "I should have guessed a girl like you would want it hard like that."

She didn't allow herself to be disappointed, because, really, what had she expected? She wasn't pretty or beautiful or sensual or sexy, damn it all. She was fun and cool, maybe, and she was definitely available. But beyond that? She was a good time, but that was it.

So she did what she always did. She put on her

good-time smile and pushed him back so he was forced to withdraw from her body.

"Always happy to be a surprise," she said, inwardly cringing. "If you'll excuse me…"

Then she hurried to the bathroom and shut the door.

# Nine

Jesus, what the hell had just happened? What had he just done?

Zeb looked down at Casey, mostly naked and flushed. Sitting on the edge of her kitchen counter. Staring at him as if she didn't know how they had gotten here.

Well, that made two of them. He felt like he was coming out of a fog—one of the thick ones that didn't just turn the world a ghostly white but blotted out the sun almost completely.

He had just taken her on her countertop. Had there even been any seduction? He tried to think but now that his blood was no longer pounding in his veins, he felt sluggish and stupid, a dull headache building in the back of his head. Hungover—that was how he felt. He didn't feel like he was in control anymore.

And he didn't like that.

He never lost control. *Ever.* He enjoyed women and sex, but this?

"If you'll excuse me," Casey said, hopping off the counter. She notched an eyebrow at him in something that looked like a challenge—but hell if he could figure out what the challenge was.

This was bad. As he watched her walk away, her body naked except for a pair of purple panties that might have matched her bra, his pulse tried to pick up the pace again. He was more than a little tempted to follow her back through her apartment, because if sex in the kitchen had been great, how good would sex in a bed be?

He was horrified to realize that he had not just had this thought but had actually taken two steps after her. He stumbled to a stop and realized that his jeans were still hanging off his butt. He tucked back into his boxer briefs and buttoned up, and the whole time, he tried to form a coherent thought.

What the hell was wrong with him? This wasn't like him. For God's sake—he hadn't even worn a condom. He had a dim recollection—she'd said she was on the Pill, right? How much had he had to drink, anyway? Three beers—that was all.

Even so, he'd done something he associated with getting plastered in a bar—he'd gone home with a woman and had wild, crazy, indiscriminate sex with her.

He scrubbed his hand over his face, but it didn't help. So he went to the sink and splashed cold water on his face. His hand—ostensibly the reason they'd come back to her place—throbbed in pain. He let the cold water run over it.

The indiscriminate sex was bad enough. But worse was that he'd just had sex with his brewmaster. An *employee*. An employee at the Beaumont Brewery, the very company he'd worked years to acquire. A company he was striving to turn around and manage productively.

And he...he couldn't even say he'd fallen into bed with Casey. They hadn't made it that far.

He splashed water on his face again. It didn't help.

He needed to think. He'd just done something he'd never done before and he wasn't sure how to handle it. Sure, he knew that employers and employees carried on affairs all the time. It happened. But it also created a ripple effect of problems. Zeb couldn't count the number of companies he'd bought that could trace their disintegration back to an affair between two adults who should have known better. And until this evening, he'd always been above such baser attractions. *Always.*

But that was before he'd met Casey. With her, he hadn't known better. And, apparently, neither had she.

Zeb found the paper towels and dried off his face. Then he scooped up his shirt and shrugged back into it. He had no idea where his hat had gone, but frankly, that was the least of his problems.

He'd lost control and gotten swept up in the moment with an employee.

It couldn't happen again.

That was the only reasonable conclusion. Yes, the sex had been amazing—but Zeb's position in the brewery and the community at large was tenuous at best. He couldn't jeopardize all of his plans for sex.

Hot, dirty, hard sex. Maybe the best sex he'd ever had. Raw and desperate and…

An involuntary shudder worked through his body. Jesus, what was *wrong* with him?

He heard the bathroom door open from somewhere inside the apartment. He could salvage this situation. He was reasonably sure that, before all the clothes had come off, she'd said…something about work. How they weren't going to do *that* at work. If he was remembering that right, then she also understood the tenuous situation they were in.

So he turned away from the sink to face her and explain, in a calm and rational way, that while what they shared had been lovely, it wasn't going to happen again.

He never got that far.

Because what he saw took his breath away and anything calm and rational was drowned out in a roar of blood rushing through his ears.

Casey had a short silk robe belted around her waist. Her hair was no longer pulled back into a ponytail—instead, it was down. Glorious waves brushed her shoulders and Zeb was almost overwhelmed with the urge to wind his fingers into that hair and pull her close to him again.

Last week, he wouldn't have called her beautiful. She still wasn't, not in the classic way. But right now, with the late-evening light filtering through the windows behind her, lighting her up with a glow, she was...

She was simply the most gorgeous woman he'd ever seen.

He was in so much trouble.

It only got worse when she smiled at him. Not the wide, friendly smile she'd aimed at every single person in the ballpark tonight. No, this was a small movement of the lips—something intimate. Something that was for him and him alone.

And then it was gone. "Can you hand me my bra?" she asked in the same voice she'd used when she'd been joking around with that beer guy.

"Sure," he said. This was good, right? This was exactly what he wanted. He didn't need her suddenly deciding she was in love with him or anything.

"Thanks." She scooped up her shirt and her jeans and disappeared again. "Do you want to try and catch the end of the game?" she called out from somewhere deeper in the apartment. Which was *not* an invitation to join her.

Zeb stood there, blinking. What the hell? Okay, so

he didn't want her to go all mushy on him. But she was acting like what had just happened…

…hadn't. Like they hadn't been flirting all night and hadn't just had some of the best sex of his life.

"Uh…" he said because seriously, what was wrong with him? First he lost control. Then he decided that this had to be a one-time-only thing. Then she appeared to be not only agreeing to the one-time thing but beating him to the punch? And that bothered him? It shouldn't have. It really shouldn't have.

But it did.

"I'll probably head back to the stadium," she said, reappearing and looking exactly the way she had when he'd first laid eyes on her this evening. Her hair was tucked back under her ball cap and she had his red cap in her hands.

It was like he hadn't left a mark on her at all.

But then he saw her swallow as she held his hat out to him. "This, um…this won't affect my job performance," she said with mock bravado.

Strangely, that made him feel better, in a perverse sort of way. He'd made an impact after all.

"It changes nothing," he agreed. He wasn't sure if his lie was any smoother than hers had been. "You're still in charge of the beer and I still want you to come up with a new product line."

*And I still want you.*

But he didn't say that part, because the signals she was sending out were loud and clear—no more touching. No more wanting.

"Okay. Good. Great." She shot him a wide smile that didn't get anywhere near her eyes.

In all his years, he'd never been in a postsex situation that was even half this awkward. Ever.

"I think I'm going to head home," he said, trying to sound just as cool as she did.

As his words hung in the air between them, something in her eyes changed and he knew that he'd hurt her.

Dammit, that wasn't what he wanted. At the very least, there'd been a moment when she'd made him feel things he hadn't thought he was capable of feeling and the sex had been electric. If nothing else, he was appreciative of those gifts she'd given him. So, even though it probably wasn't the best idea, he stepped into her and laced his fingers with hers.

"Thank you," he said in a low whisper. "I know we can't do this again—but I had a really good time tonight."

"You did?" Clearly, she didn't believe him.

"I did. The ball game and the beer and…" he cleared his throat. *And you.* But he didn't say that. "It was great. All of it." He squeezed her fingers and then, reluctantly, let go and stepped back. It was harder to do than he expected it to be. "I trust this will stay between us?"

That wasn't the right thing to say. But the hell of it was, he wasn't sure what, exactly, the right thing would be. There was no good way out of this.

"Of course," she replied stiffly. "I don't kiss and tell."

"I didn't—" He forced himself to exhale slowly. Attempting to bridge the divide between boss and lover wasn't working and he was better at being the boss anyway. "I look forward to seeing what you come up with," he said as he turned toward the door. "At work," he added stupidly.

"Right. See you at work," she said behind him as he walked out and shut the door behind him.

Just as the door closed, he thought he heard her sigh in what sounded like disappointment.

Well. He'd wondered what she'd seen when she'd looked at him.

He wished now he didn't know the answer.

All told, it could have been worse.

Her team had won and she'd gotten a bobblehead doll for Dad. She'd gotten to drink some Percheron Drafts, which were like memories in a cup. She'd gotten permission to do something similar—new, bold beers that would be hers and hers alone. None of that was bad.

Except for the part where she'd kind of, sort of, slept with her boss. And had some of the most intense orgasms of her life. And…and wanted more. She wanted more with him. More beers at the game, more short walks home, more time exploring his body with hers.

That part was not so good, because she was not going to get more.

Casey made sure to avoid the executive wing of the brewery as much as possible. It wasn't that she was avoiding Zeb, necessarily. She was just really focused on her job.

Okay, that was a total lie because she was avoiding him. But it was easy to do—in addition to overseeing the production lines, she was hiring new people and then training new people and resisting the urge to take a sledgehammer to tank fifteen because that damned piece of machinery had it coming and she had the urge to destroy something.

But underneath all of those everyday thoughts lurked two others that kept her constantly occupied. First, she had to come up with some new beers. She already had a porter in the fermenting tanks—she wanted to start with something that wasn't anywhere close to what the Beaumont Brewery currently had.

And then there was Zeb. He to be avoided at all costs. Besides, it wasn't like she wanted to see him again. She didn't. Really.

Okay, so the orgasms had been amazing. And yes, she'd had fun watching the game with him. And all right, he was simply the most gorgeous man she had ever seen, in or out of a suit.

But that didn't mean she wanted to see him again. Why would she? He had been everything she had expected—handsome, charming, great sex—and exactly nothing more than that.

She wanted him to be different. And he was—there was no argument about that. He was more intelligent, more ambitious and vastly wealthier than any other man she had ever even looked at. And that didn't even include the racial differences.

But she wanted him to be different in other ways, too. She felt stupid because she knew that, on at least one level, this was nothing but her own fault. The man had specifically asked her to tell him what she wanted—and she hadn't. Men, in her long and illustrious experience of being surrounded by them, were not mind readers. Never had been, never would be. So for her to have expected that Zeb would somehow magically guess what she needed was to feel gorgeous and beautiful and sultry—without her telling him—was unfair to both of them.

She didn't understand what was wrong with her. Why couldn't she ask for what she wanted? Why was it so hard to say that she wanted to be seduced with sweet nothings whispered in her ear? That instead of rough and dirty sex all the time, she wanted candlelight and silky negligees and—yes—bottles of champagne instead of beer? She wanted beautiful things. She wanted to *be* beautiful.

Well, one thing was clear. She was never going to get it if she didn't ask for it. Let this be a lesson, she decided. Next time a man said, *Tell me what you want,* she was going to tell him. It would be awkward and weird—but then, so was not getting what she wanted.

Next time, then. Not with her boss.

Casey wasn't sure what she expected from Zeb, but he seemed to be keeping his distance, as well. It wasn't that she wanted flowers or even a sweet little note...

Okay, that was another lie—she totally wanted flowers and the kind of love letter that she could hang on to during the long, dark winter nights. But the risk that came with any of those things showing up on her desk at work was too great. No one had ever sent her flowers at work before. If anything even remotely romantic showed up on her desk, the gossip would be vicious. Everyone would know something was up and there were always those few people in the office who wouldn't rest until they knew what they thought was the truth. And she knew damned well that if they couldn't get to the truth, they'd make up their own.

So it was fine that she avoided Zeb and he avoided her and they both apparently pretended that nothing had happened.

It was a week and a half later when she got the first email from him.

Ms. Johnson,
Status report?

Casey couldn't help but stare at her computer, her lips twisted in a grimace of displeasure. She knew she wasn't the kind of girl who got a lot of romance in her life, but really? He hadn't even signed the email, for God's sake. Four simple words that didn't seem very simple at all.

So she wrote back.

Mr. Richards, I've hired six new employees. Please see attached for their résumés. The new test beers are in process. Tank fifteen is still off-line. Further updates as events warrant.

And because she was still apparently mentally twelve, she didn't sign her email, either.

It was another day before Zeb replied.

Timeline on test beers?

Casey frowned at her email for the second time in as many days. Was he on a strict four-word diet or was she imagining things? This time, she hadn't even gotten the courtesy of a salutation.

This was fine, right? This was maintaining a professional distance with no repercussions from their one indiscretion.

Didn't feel any less awkward, though.

Still testing, she wrote back. It's going to be another few weeks before I know if I have anything.

The next day she got an even shorter email from him.

Status report?

Two words. Two stinking words and they drove her nuts. She was half-tempted to ask one of the other department heads if they got the same terse emails every day or so—but she didn't want to draw any attention to her relationship with Zeb, especially if that wasn't how he treated his other employees.

It was clear that he regretted their evening. In all reality, she should have been thankful she still had her job, because so far, she hadn't managed to handle herself as a professional around him yet. She was either yelling at him or throwing herself at him. Neither was good.

So she replied to his two-word emails that came every other day with the briefest summary she could.

Test beers still fermenting. Tank fifteen still not working. Hired a new employee—another woman.

But...

There were days when she looked at those short messages and wondered if maybe he wasn't asking something else. All she ever told him about was the beer. What if he was really asking about her?

What if *Status report?* was his really terrible way of asking, *How are you?*

What if he thought about her like she thought about him? Did he lie awake at night, remembering the feel of her hands on his body, like she remembered his? Did he think about the way he had fit against her, in her? Did he toss and turn until the frustration was too much and he had to take himself in hand—just like she had to stroke herself until a pale imitation of the climax he'd given her took the edge off?

Ridiculous, she decided. Of course he wasn't thinking about her. He'd made his position clear. They'd had a good time together once and once was enough. That was just how this went. She knew that. She was fun for a little while, but she was not the kind of woman men could see themselves in a relationship with. And to think that such a thing might be percolating just under the surface of the world's shortest emails was delusional at best. To convince herself that Zeb might actually care for her was nothing but heartache waiting to happen.

So she kept her mouth shut and went about her job, training her new employees, trying to beat tank fifteen into submission and tinkering with her new recipes. She caught evening games with her dad and added to her bobblehead collection and did her best to forget about one evening of wild abandon in Zeb Richards's arms.

Everything had gone back to normal.

*Oh, no.*

Casey stared down at the pack of birth control pills with a dawning sense of horror. Something was wrong. She hadn't been paying attention—but she was at the end of this pack. Which meant that five days ago, she should've started her period. What the hell? Why had she skipped her period?

This was *not* normal. She was regular. That was one of the advantages of being on the Pill. No surprises. No missed periods. No heart attacks at six fifty in the morning before she'd even had her coffee, for crying out loud.

In a moment of terror, she tried to recall—she hadn't skipped a dose. She had programmed a reminder into her phone. The reminder went off ten minutes after her alarm so she took a pill at exactly the same time every single day. She hadn't been sick—no antibiotics to screw with her system. Plus, she'd been on this brand for about a year.

Okay, so… She hadn't exactly had a lot of sex in the last year. Actually, now that she thought about it, there hadn't been anyone since that ballplayer a year and a half ago.

Unexpectedly, her stomach rolled and even though she hadn't had breakfast or her coffee, she raced for the bathroom. Which only made her more nervous. Was she barfing because she was panicking or was this morning sickness? Good Lord.

What if this was morning sickness?

Oh, God—what if she was…?

No, she couldn't even think it. Because if she was…

*Oh, God.*

What was she going to do?

# Ten

"Anything else?" Zeb asked Daniel.

Daniel shook his head. "The sooner we know what the new beers are going to be, the sooner we'll be able to get started on the marketing."

Zeb nodded. "I've been getting regular status updates from Casey, but I'll check in with her again."

Which wasn't exactly the truth. He had been asking for regular status updates, and like a good employee, Casey had been replying to him. The emails were short and getting shorter all the time. He was pretty sure that the last one had been two words. Nothing yet. He could almost hear her sneering them. And he could definitely hear her going, *What do you want from me?*

Truthfully, he wasn't sure. Each time he sent her an email asking for a status report, he wondered if maybe he shouldn't do something else. Ask her how she was doing, ask if things were better now that she'd hired new people.

Ask her if she'd been to many more baseball games. If she'd caught any more foul balls.

He wanted to know if she ever thought of him outside the context of beer and the brewery. If he ever drifted through her dreams like she did his.

"Well, let me know. If you thought it would help," Daniel said as he stood and began to gather his things, "I could go talk to her about the production schedule myself."

"No," Zeb said too quickly. Daniel paused and shot him a hard look. "I mean, that won't be necessary. Your time is too valuable."

For a long, painful moment, Daniel didn't say anything. "Is there something I need to know?" he asked in a voice that was too silky for its own good.

God, no. No one needed to know about that moment of insanity that still haunted him. "Absolutely not."

It was clear that Daniel didn't buy this—but he also decided not to press it. "If it becomes something I need to know about, you'll tell me, right?"

Zeb knew that Daniel had been a political consultant, even something of a fixer—more than willing to roll around in the mud if it meant getting his opponent dirty, too. The thought of Daniel doing any digging into Casey's life made Zeb more than a little uncomfortable. Plus, he had no desire to give Daniel anything he could hold over Zeb's head. This was clearly one case where sharing was not caring, brotherly bonds of love be damned.

"Certainly," Zeb said with confidence because he was certain this was not a situation Daniel needed to know anything about. His one moment of indiscretion would remain just that—a moment.

"Right," Daniel said. With that, he turned and walked out of the office.

Zeb did the same thing he'd been doing for weeks now—he sent a short email to Casey asking for a status report.

She was exactly as she had been before their indiscretion. Terse and borderline snippy, but she got the job done and done well. He had been at the brewery for only about five weeks. And in that short amount of time, Casey had already managed to goose production up by another five hundred gallons. Imagine what she could do if she ever figured out the mystery that was apparently tank fifteen.

Then, just like he did every time he thought about Casey and the night that hadn't been a date, he forced himself to stop thinking about her. Really, it shouldn't have been this hard to *not* think about her. Maybe it was the brewery, he reasoned. For so long, taking his rightful place as the CEO of the Beaumont Brewery had occupied his every waking thought. And now he'd achieved that goal. Clearly, his mind was just at…loose ends. That was all.

This did not explain why when his intercom buzzed, he was pricing tickets to the next Rockies home game. The seats directly behind Casey's were available.

"Mr. Richards?" Delores's voice crackled over the old-fashioned speaker.

"Yes?" He quickly closed the browser tab.

"Ms. Johnson is here." There was a bit of mumbling in the background that he didn't understand. "She says she has a status report for you."

Well. This was something new. It had been—what—a little over three weeks since he'd last seen her? And also, she had waited to be announced by Delores? That wasn't like her. The Casey Johnson he knew would have stormed into this office and caught him looking at baseball tickets. She would've known exactly what he was thinking, too.

So something was off. "Send her in." And then he braced for the worst.

Had she gotten another job? And if so…

If she didn't work for him anymore, would it be unethical to ask her out?

He didn't get any further than that in his thinking, because the door opened and she walked in. Zeb stood, but instantly, he could see that something was wrong. Instead of the sweaty hot mess that she frequently was during work hours, she looked pale. Her eyes were huge and for some reason, he thought she looked scared. What the hell was she scared of? Not him, that much he knew. She had never once been scared of him. And it couldn't be the last email he'd sent, either. There hadn't been anything unusual about that—it was the same basic email he'd been sending for weeks now.

"What's wrong?" He said the moment the door shut behind her.

She didn't answer right away.

"Casey?" He came out from around the desk and began to walk to her.

"I have…" Her voice shook and it just worried him all the more. She swallowed and tried again. "I have a status report for you."

She was starting to freak him out. "Is everything okay? Was there an on-the-job accident?" He tried to smile. "Did tank fifteen finally blow up?"

She tried to smile, too. He felt the blood drain out of his face at the sight of that awful grimace.

"No," she said in a voice that was a pale imitation of her normal tone. "That's not what I have a status report about."

Okay. Good. Nothing had happened on the line. "Is this about the beers?"

She shook her head, a small movement. "They're still in process. I think the porter is going to be really good."

"Excellent." He waited because there had to be a reason she was here. "Was there something else?"

Her eyes got even wider. She swallowed again. "I—"

And then the worst thing that could have possibly happened did—she squeezed her eyes shut tight and a single tear trickled down her left cheek.

It was physically painful to watch that tear. He wanted to go to her and pull her into his arms and promise that whatever had happened, he'd take care of it.

But they were at work and Delores was sitting just a few feet away. So he pushed his instincts aside. He was her boss. Nothing more. "Yes?"

The seconds ticked by while he waited. It wasn't like whatever she was trying to tell him was the end of the world, was it?

And then it was.

"I'm pregnant," she said in a shattered voice.

He couldn't even blink as his brain tried to process what she had just said. "Pregnant?" he asked as if he had never heard the word before.

She nodded. "I don't understand… I mean, I'm on the Pill—or I was. I didn't miss any. This isn't supposed to happen." Her chin quivered and another tear spilled over and ran down the side of her face.

Pregnant. She was pregnant. "And I'm the…" He couldn't even say it. *Hell.*

She nodded again. "I hadn't been with anyone in over a year." She looked up at him. "You believe me, right?"

He didn't want to. The entire thing was unbelievable.

What the hell did he know about fatherhood?

Nothing, that's what. Not a single damned thing. He'd been raised by a single mother, by a collective of women in a beauty shop. His male role models had been few and far between.

He wasn't going to be a father. Not on purpose and not by accident.

In that moment, another flash of anger hit him—but not at her. He was furious with himself. He never lost control. He never got so carried away with a woman that he couldn't even make sure that he followed the basic protocols of birth control. Except for one time.

And one time was all it took, apparently.

"You're sure?" Because this was the sort of thing that one needed to be sure about.

She nodded again. "I realized yesterday morning that I was at the end of my month of pills and I hadn't had my…" She blushed. Somehow, in the midst of a discussion about one-night stands and pregnancy, she still had the ability to look innocent. "After work yesterday, I bought a test. It was positive." Her voice cracked on that last, important word.

*Positive.*

Of all the words in the English language that had the potential to change his life, he had never figured *positive* would be the one to actually do it.

"We…" He cleared his throat. *We.* There was now a *we.* "We can't talk about this. Here." He looked around the office—his father's office. The man who had gotten his mother pregnant and paid her to leave town. "During work hours."

She looked ill. "Right. Sorry. I didn't mean to use work hours for personal business."

Dimly, he was glad to see that she still had her attitude. "We'll...we'll meet. Tonight. I can come to you."

"No," she said quickly.

"Right." She didn't want him back in her apartment, where he'd gotten carried away and gotten her into this mess. He wanted to use a less painful word—*situation, predicament*—but this was a straight-up mess. "Come to my place. At seven." She already knew where he lived. Hell, her father had done work in his house at some point.

"I don't... Jamal," she said weakly.

"Come on, Casey. We have to have this conversation somewhere and I'm sure as hell not going to have it in public. Not when you look like you're about to start sobbing and I can't even think straight."

Her eyes narrowed and he instantly regretted his words. "Of course. It's unfortunate that this upsets me," she said in a voice that could freeze fire.

"That's not what I—"

She held up her hand. "Fine. Seven, your place." She gave him a hard look—which was undercut by her scrubbing at her face with the heel of her hand. "All I ask is that you not have Jamal around." She turned and began to walk out of his office.

For some reason, he couldn't let her go. "Casey?"

She paused, her hand on the doorknob. But she didn't turn around. "What?"

"Thank you for telling me. I'm sure we can work something out."

She glanced back at him, disappointment all over her face. "Work something out," she murmured. "Well. I guess we know what kind of Beaumont you are."

Before Zeb could ask her what the hell she meant by that, she was gone.

# Eleven

"Hey, baby boy."

At the sound of his mother's voice, something unclenched in Zeb's chest. He'd screwed up—but he knew it'd work out. "Hey, Mom. Sorry to interrupt you."

"You've been quiet out there," she scolded. "Those Beaumonts giving you any trouble?"

"No." The silence had been deafening, almost. But he couldn't think about that other family right now. "It's just been busy. Taking over the company is a massive undertaking." Which was the truth. Taking over the Beaumont Brewery was easily the hardest thing he'd ever done. No, right now he had to focus on his own family. "Mom…"

She was instantly on high alert. "What's wrong?"

There wasn't a good way to have this conversation. "I'm going to be a father."

Emily Richards was hard to stun. She'd heard it all, done it all—but for a long moment, she was shocked into silence. "A baby? I'm going to be a *grandma*?"

"Yeah." Zeb dropped his head into his hands. He hadn't wanted to tell her—but he'd needed to.

This was history repeating itself. "Just like my old man, huh?"

He expected her to go off on Hardwick Beaumont, that lying, cheating bastard who'd left her high and dry. But she didn't. "You gonna buy this girl off?"

"Of course not, Mom. Come on." He didn't know what to do—but he knew what he didn't want to happen. And he didn't want to put Casey aside or buy her off.

"Are you going to take this baby away from her?"

"That's not funny." But he knew she wasn't joking. Hardwick had either paid off his babies' mothers or married and divorced them, always keeping custody.

"Baby boy…" She sighed, a sound that was disappointment and hope all together. "I want to know my grandbaby—and her mother." Zeb couldn't think of what to say. He couldn't think, period. His mother went on, "Be better than your father, Zeb. I think you know what you need to do."

Which was how Zeb wound up at a jewelry store.

He couldn't hope to make sense of what Casey had told him that morning but he knew enough to realize that he hadn't handled himself well.

Actually, no, that was letting himself off easy. In reality, he hadn't handled himself well since...the ball game. If he had realized that her getting pregnant was a legitimate outcome instead of a distant possibility...

He wanted to think that he wouldn't have slept with her. But at the very least, he wouldn't have walked out of her apartment with that disappointed sigh of hers lingering in his ears.

He'd hurt her then. He'd pissed her off today. He might not be an expert in women, but even he knew that the best solution here was diamonds.

The logic was sound. However, the fact that the diamonds he was looking at were set into engagement rings...

He was going to be a father. This thought kept coming back to him over and over again. What did he know about being a father? Nothing.

His own father had paid his mother to make sure that he never had to look at Zeb and acknowledge him as a son. Hardwick Beaumont might have been a brilliant businessman, but there was no way around the obvious fact that he'd been a terrible person. Or maybe he'd been a paragon of virtue in every area of his life except when it came to his mistresses—Emily Richards and Daniel's mother and CJ's and

God only knew how many mothers of other illegitimate children.

"Let me see that one," he said to the clerk behind the counter, pointing to a huge pear-cut diamond with smaller diamonds set in the band.

Because this was where he'd come to in his life. He was going to be a father. He'd made that choice when he'd slept with Casey. Now he had to take responsibility.

He did not want to be a father like Hardwick had been. Zeb didn't want to hide any kid of his away, denying him his birthright. If he had a child, he was going to claim that child. He was going to fight for that child, damn it all, just like his father should have fought for him. His mother wanted to know her grandbaby.

He didn't want to have to fight Casey, though. Because the simplest way to stay in his child's life was to marry the mother.

Because, really, what were the alternatives?

He could struggle through custody agreements and legal arrangements—all of which would be fodder for gossip rags. He could pretend he hadn't slept with his brewmaster and put his own child through the special kind of hell that was a childhood divorced from half his heritage. He could do what Hardwick had done and cut a check to ensure his kid was well cared for—and nothing more.

Or he could ask Casey to marry him. Tonight. It

would be sudden and out of left field and she might very well say no.

Married. He'd never seen himself married. But then, he'd never seen himself as a father, either. One fifteen-minute conversation this afternoon and suddenly he was an entirely different person, one he wasn't sure he recognized. He stared at the engagement ring, but he was seeing a life where he and Casey were tied together both by a child and by law.

No, not just that. By more than that. There was more between them than just a baby. So much more.

He'd spend his days with her watching baseball and discussing beer and—hopefully—having great sex. And the kid—he knew Casey would be good with the kid. She'd be the kind of mom who went to practices and games. She'd be fun, hands-on.

As for Zeb...

Well, he had two different businesses to run. He had to work. He'd made a fortune—but fortunes could be lost as fast as they'd been made. He'd seen it happen. And he couldn't let it happen to him. More than that, he couldn't let it happen to Casey. To their family.

He had to take care of them. Hardwick Beaumont had cut Emily Richards a check and the money had been enough to take care of him when he'd been a baby—but it hadn't lasted forever. His mother had needed to work to make ends meet. She'd worked days, nights, weekends.

There had been times when Zeb wondered if she

was avoiding him. Emily Richards had always been happy to foist child care off on the other stylists and the customers. No one minded, but there'd been times he'd just wanted his mom and she'd been too busy.

He couldn't fault her drive. She was a self-made woman. But she'd put her business ahead of him, her own son. Even now, Zeb had trouble talking to her without feeling like he was imposing upon her time.

He didn't want that for his child. He wanted more for his family. He didn't want his baby's mother to miss out on all the little things that made up a childhood. He didn't want to miss them, either—but not only was the brewery his legacy, it would be his child's, as well. He *couldn't* let the brewery slide.

He'd work hard, as he always had. But he would be there. Part of his child's life. Maybe every once in a while, he'd even make it for a game or a play or whatever kids did in school. And he'd have Casey by his side.

"I'll take it," he said, even though he wasn't sure what he was looking at anymore. But he'd take that life, with Casey and their child.

"It's a beautiful piece." A deep voice came from his side.

Zeb snapped out of his reverie and turned to find himself face-to-face with none other than Chadwick Beaumont. For a long moment, Zeb did nothing but stare. It wasn't like looking in a mirror. Chadwick was white, with sandy blond hair that he wore a little long and floppy. But despite that, there were things Zeb recognized—the jawline and the eyes.

Zeb's green eyes had marked him as different in the African American community. But here? Here, standing with this man he had never seen up close before, his eyes marked him as something else. They marked him as one of the Beaumonts.

Chadwick stuck out his hand. "I'm Chadwick."

"Zeb," he said, operating on autopilot as his hand went out to give Chadwick's a firm shake. "And who's this?" he asked, trying to smile at the little girl Chadwick was holding.

"This is my daughter, Catherine."

Zeb studied the little girl. She couldn't be more than a year and a half old. "Hi there, Catherine," he said softly. He looked at Chadwick. "I didn't realize I was an uncle." The idea seemed so foreign to him that it was almost unrecognizable.

The little girl turned her face away and into Chadwick's neck—then, a second later, she turned back, peeking at Zeb through thick lashes.

"You are—Byron has two children. Technically, Catherine is my wife's daughter from a previous relationship. But I've adopted her." Chadwick patted his daughter on her back. "I found that, when it comes to being a Beaumont, it's best to embrace a flexible definition of the word *family*."

An awkward silence grew between them because Zeb didn't quite know what to say to that. He'd always thought that, at some point, he would confront the Beaumonts. In his mind's eye, the confrontation was not nearly this…polite. There wouldn't be any chitchat. He would revel in what he had done, taking the company away from them and punishing them for failing to acknowledge him and they would…cower or beg for forgiveness. Or something.

There was a part of him that still wanted that— but not in the middle of a high-end jewelry store and not in front of a toddler.

So instead, he didn't say anything. He had no idea what he was even supposed to say as he looked at this man who shared his eyes.

Suddenly, Zeb desperately wanted to know what kind of man this brother of his was. More specifically, he wanted to know what kind of man Casey thought Chadwick was. Because Zeb still didn't know if he was like his father or his brother and he needed to know.

"Who's the lucky woman?" Chadwick asked.

"Excuse me?"

Just then the clerk came back with the small bag that held an engagement ring. Chadwick smiled. "The ring. Anyone I know?"

It took a lot to make Zeb blush, but right then his face got hot. Instead of responding, he went on the offensive. "What about you?"

Chadwick smiled again, but this time it softened everything about his face. Zeb recognized that look—and it only got stronger when Chadwick leaned down and pressed a kiss to the top of his daughter's head. It was the look of love. "My wife is expecting again and the pregnancy has been…tiring. I'm picking her up something because, really, there's nothing else I can do and diamonds tend to make everything better. Wouldn't you agree?"

"Congratulations," Zeb said automatically. But he didn't tell this man that he'd had the exact same thought. He only hoped he wasn't wrong about the diamonds.

"Will there be anything else?" The clerk asked in a super-perky voice.

Zeb and Chadwick turned to see her looking at them with bright eyes and a wide smile. Crap. He needed to have a conversation with Chadwick— even if he wasn't exactly sure what the conversation should be about. But it couldn't happen here. How much longer before someone put two and two together and there were cameras or news crews and reporters or cell-phone-toting gossipmongers crowding them? Zeb didn't want to deal with it himself— he couldn't imagine that Chadwick wanted to put his daughter through it, either.

"No," he said just as another clerk approached and handed a small bag to Chadwick.

"Your necklace, Mr. Beaumont," the second clerk said. She and the first clerk stood elbow to elbow, grinning like loons.

They had to get out of here right now. "Would you like to…" *continue this conversation elsewhere? But* he didn't even get that far before Chadwick gave a quick nod of his head.

Both men picked up their small bags and headed out of the store. When they were safely away from the eager clerks, Zeb bit the bullet and asked first. "Would you like to go get a drink or something?"

"I wish I could," Chadwick said in a regretful voice. "But I don't think any conversation we have should be in public. And besides," he went on, switching his daughter to his other arm, "we probably only have another half an hour before we have a meltdown."

"Sure," Zeb said, trying to keep the disappointment out of his voice.

Chadwick stopped, which made Zeb stop, too. "You want answers." It was not a question.

*Yes.* "I don't want to intrude on your family time."

Chadwick stared at Zeb for a moment longer and his face cracked with the biggest smile that Zeb had ever seen. "You *are* family, Zeb."

That simple statement made Zeb feel as if someone had just gut-shot him. It took everything he had not to double over. This man considered *him* family? There was such a sense of relief that appeared out of nowhere—

But at the same time, Zeb was angry. If he was family, why hadn't Chadwick seen fit to inform him of that before now? Why had he waited until a chance meeting in a jewelry store, for God's sake?

Chadwick's eyes cut behind Zeb's shoulder. "We

need to keep moving." He began walking again and Zeb had no choice but to follow. They headed out toward the parking lot.

Finally, Zeb asked, "How long have you known? About me, I mean."

"About six years. After my…" He winced. "I mean *our* father—"

Zeb cut him off. "He wasn't my father. Not really."

Chadwick nodded. "After Hardwick died," he went on diplomatically, "it took me a while to stabilize the company and get my bearings. I'd always heard rumors about other children and when I finally got to the point where I had a handle on the situation, I hired an investigator."

"Did you know about Daniel before the press conference?"

Chadwick nodded. "And Carlos."

That brought Zeb up short. CJ was not as unfindable as he liked to think he was. "He prefers CJ."

Chadwick smirked. "Duly noted. And of course, we already knew about Matthew. There was actually a bit of a break after that. I don't know if Hardwick got tired of paying off his mistresses or what."

"Are there more of us? Because I could only find the other two."

Chadwick nodded again. "There are a few that are still kids. The youngest is thirteen. I'm in contact with his mother, but she has decided that she's not interested in introducing her son to the family. I provide a monthly stipend—basically, I pay child support for the other three children." They reached a fancy SUV with darkened windows. "It seems like the least I can do, after everything Hardwick did." He opened up the back door and slid his daughter into the seat.

As he buckled in the little girl, Zeb stared at Chadwick in openmouthed shock. "You...you pay child support? For your half siblings?"

"They are family," Chadwick said simply as he clicked the buckle on the child seat. He straightened and turned to face Zeb. But he didn't add anything else. He just waited.

*Family.* It was such an odd concept to him. He had a family—his mother and the larger community that had orbited around her salon. He had Jamal. And now, whether she liked it or not, he had Casey, too.

"Why didn't you contact me?" He had so many questions, but that one was first. Chadwick was taking care of the other bastards. Why not him?

"By the time I found you, we were both in our thirties. You'd built up your business on your own, and at the time, I didn't think you wanted anything to do with us." Chadwick shrugged. "I didn't realize until later how wrong I was."

"What kind of man was he?" Zeb asked. And he felt wrong, somehow, asking it—but he needed to know. He was getting a very good idea of what kind of man Chadwick was—loyal, dependable, the kind of man who would pay child support for his siblings because they were family, whether they liked it or not. The kind of man who not only cared about his wife but bought her diamonds because she was tired. The kind of man who knew how to put his own daughter into a safety seat.

Zeb knew he couldn't be like Chadwick, but he was beginning to understand what Casey meant when she asked if Zeb was like his brother.

Chadwick sighed and looked up at the sky. It was getting late, but the sun was still bright. "Why don't you come back to the house? This isn't the sort of thing that we can discuss in a parking lot."

Zeb just stared at the man. His brother. Chadwick had made the offer casually, as if it were truly no big deal. Zeb was family and family should come home and have a beer. Simple.

But it wasn't. Nothing about this was simple.

Zeb held up his small jewelry bag with the engagement ring that he somehow had to convince Casey to wear. "I have something to do at seven." He braced himself for Chadwick to ask about who the lucky woman was again, but the question didn't come.

Instead, Chadwick answered Zeb's earlier question. "Hardwick Beaumont..." He sighed and closed the door, as if he were trying to shield his daughter from the truth. "He was a man of contradictions—but then again, I'm sure we all are." He paused. "He was... For me, he was hard. He was a hard man. He was a perfectionist and when I couldn't give him perfection..." Chadwick grimaced.

"Was he violent?"

"He could be. But I think that was just with me, because I was his heir. He ignored Phillip almost completely, but then Frances—his first daughter—he spoiled her in every sense of the word." Chadwick tried to smile, but it looked like a thing of pain. "You asked me why I hadn't contacted you earlier—well, the truth is, I think I was a little jealous of you."

*"What?"* Surely, Zeb hadn't heard correctly. Surely, his brother, the heir of the Beaumont fortune, had not just said that he was—

"Jealous," Chadwick confirmed. "I'm not exaggerating when I say that Hardwick screwed us all up. I…" He took a deep breath and stared up at the night sky again. "He was my father, so I couldn't hate him, but I don't think I loved him, either. And I don't think he loved us. Certainly not me. So when I found out about you and the others, how you'd spent your whole lives without Hardwick standing over you, threatening and occasionally hitting you, I was jealous. You managed to make yourself into a respected businessman on your own. You did what you wanted—not what *he* wanted. It's taken me most of my life to separate out what I want from what he demanded."

Zeb was having trouble processing this information. "And I spent years trying to get what you have," he said, feeling numb. Years of believing that he had been cut out of his rightful place next to Hardwick Beaumont. It had never occurred to him that perhaps he didn't want to be next to Hardwick Beaumont.

Because he could see in Chadwick's eyes that this was the truth. His father had been a terrible man. Sure, Zeb had known that—a good man did not buy off his mistress and send her packing. A good man did not pretend like he didn't have multiple children hidden away. A good man took care of his family, no matter what.

Zeb suddenly had no idea if he was a good man or not. He took care of his mother, even when she drove him nuts, and he looked out for Jamal, the closest thing he'd had to a brother growing up.

But the Beaumonts were his family, too. Instead of looking out for them, he'd done everything he could to undermine them.

He realized Chadwick was staring. "I'm sorry," Chadwick said quickly. "You look like him."

Zeb snorted. "I look like my mother."

"I know." Chadwick moved a hand, as if he were going to pat Zeb on the shoulder—but he didn't. Instead, he dropped his arm back to his side. Then he waited. Zeb appreciated the silence while he tried to put his thoughts in order.

He knew he was running out of time. Chadwick's daughter would sit quietly for only so long—either that, or someone with a camera would show up. But he had so many questions. And he wasn't even sure that the answers would make it better.

For the first time in his life, he wasn't sure that knowing more was a good thing.

"I don't know how much of it was PR," Chadwick

suddenly began. "But the press conference was brilliant and I wanted to let you know that we're glad to see that the brewery is back in family hands."

*Really?* But Zeb didn't let his surprise at this statement show. "We're still competitors," he replied. "Casey is formulating a line of beers to compete directly with Percheron Drafts as we speak."

Chadwick notched an eyebrow at him. "She'll be brilliant at it," he said, but with more caution in his voice. Too late, Zeb realized that he had spoken of her with too much familiarity. "And I expect nothing less—from both of you."

Inside the car, the little girl fussed. "I have to get going," Chadwick said, and this time, he did clap Zeb on the shoulder. "Come to the house sometime. We'll have dinner. Serena would love to meet you."

Zeb assumed that was Chadwick's wife. "What about the rest of your brothers and sisters?"

"You mean *our* brothers and sisters. They're... curious, shall we say. But getting all of us together in one room can be overwhelming. Besides, Serena was my executive assistant at the brewery. She knows almost as much about the place as I do."

Zeb stared at him. "You married your assistant?" Because that seemed odd, somehow. This seemed like something their father would've done. Well, maybe not the marrying part.

Had his brother gotten his assistant pregnant and then married her? Was history repeating itself? Was it possible for history to repeat itself even if Zeb hadn't known what that history was?

Chadwick gave him a look that might've intimidated a lesser man. But not Zeb. "I try not to be my father," he said in a voice that was colder than Zeb had heard yet. "But it seemed to be a family trait—falling for our employees. I married my assistant. Phillip married a horse trainer he hired. Frances married the last CEO of the brewery."

Oh, God. Had he somehow managed to turn into his father without ever even knowing a single thing about the man? He had gotten Casey pregnant because when he was around her, he couldn't help himself. She'd taken all of his prized control and blown it to smithereens, just as if she'd been blowing foam off a beer.

"Hardwick Beaumont is dead," Chadwick said with finality. "He doesn't have any more power over me, over any of us." He looked down at the small bag Zeb still clutched in his hand. "We are known for our control—both having it and losing it. But it's not the control that defines us. It's how we deal with the consequences."

Inside the car, the toddler started to cry in earnest. "Come by sometime," Chadwick said as he stuck out his hand. "I look forward to seeing how you turn the brewery around."

"I will," Zeb said as they shook hands.

"If you have any other questions, just ask."

Zeb nodded and stood aside as Chadwick got

into his vehicle and drove away—back to the family home, to his assistant and their children. Back to where he could be his own man, without having to prove anything to his father ever again.

Hardwick Beaumont was dead. Suddenly, years of plotting and planning, watching and waiting for an opportunity to take revenge against the Beaumonts—was it all for nothing?

Because Zeb wasn't sure he wanted revenge—not on his brothers. Not anymore. How could he? If they'd known of him for only six years—hell, six years ago, Zeb had been just moving to New York, just taking ZOLA to the next level. What would he have done, six years ago? He wouldn't have given up ZOLA. He would've been suspicious of any overtures that Chadwick might've made. He wouldn't have wanted to put himself in a position where any Beaumont had power over him. And then he wouldn't have been in a position to take the brewery back from the corporation that bought it.

And now? Now Chadwick wanted him to succeed? Even though they were competitors—and nowhere near friends—he hoped that Zeb would turn the brewery around?

It was damned hard to get revenge against a dead man. And Zeb wasn't sure he wanted revenge against the living.

He looked down at the small bag with an engagement ring in it.

What did he want?

# Twelve

**W**hat did she want?

Casey had been asking herself that exact question for hours now. And the answer hadn't changed much.

She had no idea.

Well, that wasn't entirely the truth. What she wanted was… God, it sounded so silly, even in her head. But she wanted something romantic to happen. The hell of it was, she didn't know exactly what that was. She wanted Zeb to pull her into his arms and promise that everything was going to be all right. And not just the general promise, either. She wanted specific promises. He was going to take care of her and the baby. He was going to be a good father. He was going to be…

Seriously, they didn't have a whole lot of a relationship here. She didn't even know if she wanted to have a relationship—beyond the one that centered around a child, of course. Sometimes she did and sometimes she didn't. He was so gorgeous—too gorgeous. Zeb wasn't the kind of guy she normally went for; he was cool and smooth. Plus, he was a Beaumont. As a collective, they weren't known for being the most faithful of husbands.

That was unfair to Chadwick. But it wasn't unfair enough to Hardwick.

Fidelity aside, she had absolutely no idea if Zeb could be the kind of father she wanted her child to have. It wasn't that her own father, Carl Johnson, was perfect—he wasn't. But he cared. He had *always* cared for Casey, fighting for her and protecting her and encouraging her to do things that other people wouldn't have supported.

That was what she wanted. She wanted to do that for her and for this child.

Based on Zeb's reaction in the office earlier? She didn't have a lot of faith.

Casey had not been the best of friends with Chadwick Beaumont. They had been coworkers who got along well, and he'd never seen her as anything more than one of the guys. Which was fine. But she knew all of the office gossip—he had fallen in love with his assistant just as Serena Chase had gotten pregnant with someone else's baby. He had given up the company for her and adopted the baby girl as his own. Hell, even Ethan Logan—who had not understood a damned thing about beer—had given up the company for Frances Beaumont because they'd fallen in love.

Zeb's entire reason for being in Denver was the brewery.

Besides, she didn't want him to give it up. In fact, she preferred not to give it up, either. She had no idea what the company's maternity-leave policy looked like, though. She didn't know if Larry could handle the production lines while she was away. And after the leave was over, she didn't know how she would be a working mother with a newborn.

She didn't know if she would have to make it work herself or if she'd have help. And she still didn't know what she wanted that help to look like. But she didn't want to give up her job. She'd worked years to earn her place at the brewery's table. She loved being a brewmaster. It was who she was.

She was running a little bit late by the time she made it to the mansion where Zeb had set up shop. As she got out of her car, she realized her hands were shaking. Okay, everything was shaking. Was it too early to start blaming things on hormones? God, she had no idea. She hadn't spent a lot of time around babies and small children growing up. Other girls got jobs as babysitters. She went to work as an electrical assistant for her father. Small children were a mystery to her.

*Oh, God.* And now she was going to have one.

Stuck in this tornado of thoughts, she rang the bell. She knew she needed to tell Zeb what she wanted. Hadn't she resolved that she was going to do better at that? Okay, that resolution had been specifically about sex—but the concept held. Men were not mind readers. She needed to tell him what she wanted to happen here.

All she had to do in the next thirty seconds was figure out what that was.

It wasn't even thirty seconds before the door opened and there stood Zeb, looking nothing like the CEO she'd seen in the office just a few hours ago. But he didn't look like the sports fan that she'd gone on an almost date with, either. He was something in the middle. His loose-fitting black T-shirt hinted at his muscles, instead of clinging to them. It made him look softer. Easier to be around. God, how she needed him to be easier right now.

"Hi," she croaked. She cleared her throat and tried to smile.

"Come in," he said in a gentle voice. Which was, all things considered, a step up from this morning's reaction.

He shut the door behind her and then led her through the house. It was massive, a maze of rooms and parlors and stairs. He led her to a room that could best be described as a study—floor-to-ceiling bookcases, a plush Persian rug, heavy leather furniture and a fireplace. It was ornate, in a manly sort of way. And, thankfully, it was empty.

Zeb shut the door behind her and then they were alone. She couldn't bring herself to sit—she had too much nervous energy. She forced herself to stand in the middle of the room. "This is nice."

"Jamal can take the credit." Zeb gave her a long look and then he walked toward her. She hadn't actually seen him for several weeks—outside of this morning, of course. Was it possible she had forgotten how intense it was being in Zeb Richards's sights? "How are you?" he asked as he got near.

"Well, I'm pregnant."

He took another step closer and she tensed. Right about now it would be great if she could figure out what she wanted. "I don't mean this to sound callous," he said, lifting his hands in what looked a hell of a lot like surrender, "but I thought you said you were on the Pill?"

"I am. I mean, I was. I diagnosed myself via the internet—these things can…happen. It's something called breakthrough ovulation, apparently." He was another step closer and even though neither of them were making any broad declarations of love, her body was responding to his nearness all the same.

She could feel a prickle of heat starting low on her back and working its way up to her neck. Her cheeks were flushing and, God help her, all she wanted was for him to wrap his arms around her and tell her that everything was going to be all right.

And then, amazingly, that was exactly what happened. Zeb reached her and folded his strong arms around her and pulled her against the muscles of his chest and held her. "These things just happen, huh?"

With a sigh, she sank into his arms. This probably wasn't a good idea. But then, anything involving her touching Zeb Richards was probably a bad idea. Because once she started touching him, it was just too damn hard to stop. "Yeah."

"I'm sorry it happened to you."

She needed to hear that—but what killed her was the sincerity in his voice. Her eyes began to water. Oh, no—she didn't want to cry. She wasn't a crier. Really. She was definitely going to blame that one on the hormones.

"What are we going to do?" she asked. "I haven't seen you in weeks. We had one almost date and everything about it was great except that it ended... awkwardly. And since then..."

"Since then," he said as she could feel his voice rumbling deep out of his chest. It shouldn't have been soothing, dammit. She wanted to keep her wits about her, but he was lulling her into a sense of warmth and security. "Since then I've thought of you constantly. I wanted to see you but I got the feeling you might not have reciprocated that desire."

*What?* "Is that why you've been sending me emails every day?" She leaned back and looked up at him. "Asking for status reports?"

Oh, God, that blush was going to be the death of her. If there was one thing she knew, it was that an adorable Zeb Richards was an irresistible Zeb Richards. "You said at work that it was all about the beer. So I was trying to keep it professional."

Even as he said it, though, he was backing her up until they reached one of the overstuffed leather couches. Then he was pulling her down onto his lap and curling his arms around her and holding her tight. "But we're not at work right now, are we?"

She sighed into him. "No, we're not. We can't even claim that this is a corporate outing."

He chuckled and ran his hand up and down her back. She leaned into his touch because it was what she wanted. And she hadn't even had to ask for it. She let herself relax into him and wrapped her arms around his neck. "What are we going to do, Zeb?"

His hand kept moving up and down and he began rubbing his other hand along the side of her thigh. "I'm going to take care of you," he said, his voice soft and close to her ear.

God, it was what she needed to hear. She knew she was strong and independent. She lived her life on her own terms. She'd gotten the job she wanted and a nice place close to the ballpark. She paid her bills on time and managed to sock some away for retirement.

But this? Suddenly, her life was not exactly her own anymore and she didn't know how to deal with it.

"There's something between us," Zeb said, his breath caressing her cheek. She turned her face toward him. "I feel it. When I'm around you…" He cupped her face in his hands. "I could fall for you."

Her heart began to pound. "I feel it, too," she whispered, her lips moving against his. "I'm not supposed to go for someone like you. You're my boss and everything about this is wrong. So why can't I help myself?"

"I don't know. But I don't think I want you to."

And then he was kissing her. Unlike the first time, which had been hurried and frantic, this was everything she dreamed a kiss could be. Slowly, his lips moved over hers as he kissed the corner of her mouth and then ran his tongue along her lower lip.

If she'd been able to help herself, she wouldn't have opened her lips for him, wouldn't have drawn his tongue into her mouth, wouldn't have run her hands over his hair. If she'd been able to help herself at all, she wouldn't have moaned into his mouth when he nipped at her lip, her neck, her earlobe.

"I want you in a bed this time," he said when she skimmed her hands over his chest and went to grab the hem of his shirt. "I want to strip you bare and lay you out and I want to show you exactly what I can do for you."

"Yes," she gasped. And then she gasped again when he stood, lifting her in his arms as if she weighed next to nothing.

"Casey," he said as he stood there, holding her. His gaze stroked over her face. "Have I ever told you how beautiful you are?"

# Thirteen

Whatever he'd just said, he needed to make sure he said it again. Often.

Because suddenly, Casey was all over him. She kissed him with so much passion he almost had to sit down on the couch again so he could strip her shirt off her and sink into her soft body and…

He slammed on the brakes. That wasn't what he'd promised her. Bed. He needed to get to a bed. And at the rate they were going, he needed to get there quickly.

It would be so tempting to get lost in her body. She had that ability, to make him lose himself. But it was different now. Everything was different. She was carrying his child. This wasn't about mindless pleasure, not anymore.

It wasn't like he wanted to be thinking about Chadwick Beaumont right now, but even as he carried Casey out of the office and up the wide staircase to his suite of rooms, he couldn't stop replaying some of the things his brother had said.

Casey took Zeb's hard-won control and blew it to smithereens, but that wasn't what made him a Beaumont. It was what he did after that.

He could turn her away. He could set her up with a monthly stipend and let her raise their child, just as Chadwick was doing with some of their half siblings.

But that was what his father would do. And Zeb knew now that he did not want to be like that man. And what was more, he didn't *have* to be like his father. He wasn't sure he could be as selfless as his brother was—but he didn't have to be that way, either.

He could be something else. Someone else. Someone who was both a Beaumont *and* a Richards.

A sense of rightness filled him. It was right that he take Casey to bed—a real bed this time. It was right that he make love to her tonight, tomorrow—maybe even for the rest of their lives. It was right that he become a part of the Beaumont family by *making* himself a part of it—both by finally taking his place as the head of the brewery and by starting his own family.

It was right to be here with Casey. To marry her and take care of her and their baby.

He kicked open the door to a suite of rooms and

carried her through. Why was this house so damned big? Because he had to pass through another room and a half before he even got anywhere near his bed and each step was agony. He was rock hard and she was warm and soft against him and all he wanted to do was bury himself in her again and again.

Finally, he made it to his bed. Carefully, he set her down on top of the covers. He was burning for her as he lowered himself down on top of her—gently, this time. He knew that just because she was a few weeks along, didn't mean she was now some impossibly fragile, delicate flower who would snap if he looked at her wrong. But he wanted to treat her with care.

So, carefully, he slipped her T-shirt over her head. He smiled down at her plain beige bra. "No purple today?"

"I didn't wear my lucky bra, because I didn't think I was going to get lucky," she said in a husky voice. This time, when she grabbed at the hem of his shirt, he didn't stop her.

He wanted to take this slow, but when she ran her hands over his chest, her fingernails lightly grazing his nipples, she took what little self-control he had left and blew it away. Suddenly, he was undoing her jeans and yanking them off and she was grabbing his and trying to push them off his hips.

"Zeb…" she said, and he heard the need for him in her voice.

His blood was pounding in his veins—and other places—but he had to prove to her that he could be good for her. So instead of falling into her body, he knelt in front of the bed and, grabbing her by the hips, pulled her to the edge of it.

"I'm going to take care of you," he promised. He had never meant the words more than he did right now.

Last time, he hadn't even gotten her panties off her. Last time, he'd been more than a little selfish. This time, however, it was all about her.

He lowered his mouth to her sex and was rewarded as a ripple of tension moved through her body.

"Oh," she gasped as he spread her wide and kissed her again and again.

With each touch, her body spasmed around him. She ran her hand over his hair, heightening his awareness. Everything was about her. All he could see and taste and touch and smell and hear was her. Her sweetness was on his tongue and her moans were in his ears and her soft skin was under his hands.

Last time, he hadn't done this—taking the time to learn her. But this time? Every touch, every sigh, was a lesson—one he committed to memory.

This was right. The connection he felt with her— because that was what it was, a connection—it was something he'd never had before. He'd spent the last three weeks trying to ignore it, but he was done with that. He wasn't going to lie to himself anymore.

He wanted her. And by God, he was going to have her.

He slipped a finger inside her and her hips came off the bed as she cried out. "Zeb!"

"Let me show you what I can do for you," he murmured against her skin. "God, Casey—you're so beautiful."

"Yes, yes—don't stop!"

So he didn't. He stroked his tongue over her sex and his fingers into her body and told her again and again how beautiful she was, how good she felt around him. And the whole time, he got harder and harder until he wasn't sure he could make it. He needed her to let go so that he could let go.

Finally, he put his teeth against her sex—just a small nip, not a true bite. But that was what it took. Something a little bit raw and a little bit hard in the middle of something slow and sensual. She needed both.

Luckily, he could give her that. He could give her anything she wanted.

Her body tensed around him and her back came off the bed as the orgasm moved through her. Even he couldn't hold himself back anymore. The last of his control snapped and he let it carry him as he surged up onto the bed, between her legs. "You are so beautiful when you come," he said as he joined his body to hers.

Everything else fell away. His messy family history and their jobs, baseball and status reports—none of that mattered. All that mattered was that Casey was here with him and there was something between them and they couldn't fight it. Not anymore.

She cried out again as a second orgasm took her and he couldn't hold back anything else. His own climax took him and he slammed his mouth down over hers. If this was the rest of his life, he could be a happy man.

Suddenly exhausted, he collapsed onto her. She wrapped her arms around his back and held him to her. "Wow, Zeb," she murmured in his ear.

"I forgot to ask about birth control that time." She laughed at that, which made him smile. He managed to prop himself up on his elbows to look down at her. "Casey—" he said, but then he stopped because he suddenly realized he was about to tell her that he thought he was in love with her.

She stroked her fingertips over his cheek. "That…" she said, and he could hear the happiness in her voice. "That was everything I have ever dreamed." There was a pause. "And maybe a few things I hadn't thought of yet."

It was his turn to laugh. "Just think, after we're married, we get to do that every night." He withdrew from her body and rolled to the side, pulling her into his arms.

"What?" She didn't curl up in his arms like he thought she would.

"I'm going to take care of you," he told her again, pulling her into him. "I didn't have the chance to tell you, but I ran into Chadwick this afternoon and talking with him cleared up a couple of things for me."

"It...did?"

"It did. You've asked me if I'm like my father or my brother and I didn't know either of them. I only knew what was public knowledge. I knew that my father was not a good man, because he paid my mother to disappear. And I knew that everyone at the brewery liked Chadwick. But that didn't tell me what I needed to know."

"What did you need to know?" Her voice sounded oddly distant. Maybe she was tired from the sex?

That he could understand. His own eyelids were drifting shut but he forced himself to think for a bit longer. "When you asked me which one I was like, you were really asking me if I could be a good man. And not just a good man—a good man for you. I understand what that means now. You need someone who's loyal, who will take care of you and our child. You need someone who appreciates you the way you are."

Then she did curl into him. She slung her arm around his waist and held him tight. "Yes," she whispered against skin. "Yes, that's what I need."

"And that's what I want to give you." He disentangled himself long enough to reach over the side of the bed and retrieve his pants. He pulled out the small velvet-covered box with the ring inside. "I want to marry you and take care of you and our baby together. You won't have to struggle with being a single mother or worrying about making ends meet—I'll take care of all of that."

She stared at the box. "How do you mean?"

Was it his imagination or did she sound cautious? They were past that. He was all in. This was the right thing to do. He was stepping up and taking care of his own—her and their child.

"Obviously, we can't keep working together and you're going to need to take it easy. And your apartment was cute, but it's not big enough for the three of us." He hugged her. "I know I haven't talked about my childhood a lot—it was fine, but it was rough, too. My mom—she worked all the time and I basically lived at the salon, with a whole gaggle of employees watching over me. All I knew was that my dad didn't want me and my mom was working. And I don't want that kind of life for our baby. I don't want us to pass the baby off to employees or strangers. I want us to do this right."

"But...but I have to work, Zeb."

"No, you don't—don't you see? We'll get married and you can stay home—here. I'll take care of everything. We can be a family. And I can get to know Chadwick and his family—my family, I mean. All of the Beaumonts. I don't have to show them that I'm better than them. Because I think maybe..." He sighed. "Maybe they're going to accept me just the way I am, too."

He still couldn't believe that was possible. His whole life, he'd never felt completely secure in his own skin. He was either too light or too black, stuck in a no-man's-land in between.

But here in Denver? Chadwick wished him well and had invited him to be part of the family. And all Casey cared about was that he accepted her the exact same way he wanted to be accepted.

Finally, he had come home.

He opened the box and took the ring out. "Marry me, Casey. I know it's quick but I think it's the right thing."

She sat up and stared at him. "Wait— I— *Wait.*"

He looked at her, confused. "What?"

A look of dawning horror crossed over her face— a look that was not what any man wanted to see after sex that good and a heartfelt offer of marriage. "You want to marry me so I can stay home and raise our kid?"

"Well…yes. I don't want to be the kind of father my own father was. I want to be part of my kid's life. I want to be part of your life. And I don't want you to struggle like my mom did. You mean too much to me to let that happen."

And then, suddenly, she was moving. She rolled out of the bed and away from him, gathering up her clothes.

"Are you serious?" she said, and he heard a decided note of panic in her voice. "That's not what I want."

"What do you mean, it's not what you want? I

thought we agreed—there was something between us and you're pregnant and this makes sense."

"This does *not* make sense," she said as she angrily jabbed her legs into her jeans. "I am not about to quit my job so I can stay home and raise your baby."

"Casey—wait!" But she was already through the first door. She didn't even have a shirt on yet. She was running away as fast as she could.

Zeb threw himself out of bed, the engagement ring still in his hand. "Casey!" he called after her. "Talk to me, dammit. What is your problem here? I thought this would work. There's something here and I don't want to let that go." Unless...

Something new occurred to him. She had given him every indication that she wanted the baby, even if it was unexpected. But what if...?

What if she didn't? What if she didn't want to read stories at night and teach their kid how to ride a bike or throw a baseball? What if she didn't want to be the hands-on mom he'd imagined, coaching T-ball and playing in the park? The kind of mother he didn't have.

What if she was going to be like his mother—distant and reserved and...*bitter* about an unplanned pregnancy?

She swung around on him, her eyes blazing. "You don't know what you're talking about," she shot at him. The words sliced through the air like bullets out of a gun. "I don't want to quit my job. I've never wanted to be a stay-at-home mom."

"But you can't keep working," he told her, pushing against the rising panic in his chest. "You shouldn't have to."

That was the wrong thing to say. "I don't *have* to do anything I don't want to do. After I have this baby, I'm going to need help. If you think I'm going to give up my job and my life and fit myself into your world just because I'm pregnant with your baby, you've got another think coming."

She spun again and stalked away from him. "Casey!" He sprinted after her and managed to catch up to her—but only because she was trying to get her shirt on. "I'm trying to do the right thing here."

He was horrified to see tears spill over her eyelids. "Is this how it's going to be? Every time we're together, you make me feel so good—and then you ruin it. You just ruin it, Zeb." She scrubbed her hand across her face. "You'll be all perfect and then you'll be a total jerk."

What the hell was she talking about? "I'm trying not to be a jerk. I thought a marriage proposal and a commitment was the right thing to do. Obviously, we can't keep working together, because we can't keep our hands off each other." Her cheeks blushed a furious red. But then again, everything about her was furious right now. "So this is the obvious solution. I'm *not* going to raise a bastard. You *are* going to marry me. We *will* raise our child together and, damn it all, we *will* be a happy family. Unless…" He swallowed. "Unless you don't want me?"

She looked at him like he was stupid. Happiness seemed a long way off. She hadn't even put her bra on—it was hanging from her hand.

"You are trying so hard not to be like your father—but this? Telling me what I want? Telling me what I'm going to do without giving me an option? You're essentially firing me. You're going to put me in this house and make me completely dependent upon you. You're going to hide me away here under the pretense of taking care of me because you somehow think that's going to absolve you of any guilt you feel. And that?" She jabbed at his chest with a finger. "That is *exactly* what your father would've done."

Her words hit him like a sledgehammer to the chest, so hard that he physically stumbled backward.

"I am not trying to hide anyone away. I'm not ashamed of you!" He realized too late he was shouting but he couldn't stop. "I just want my kid to have something I didn't—two loving parents who give a damn about whether he lives or dies!"

Her face softened—but only a little bit. She still looked fierce and when she spoke, it was in a low voice that somehow hurt all the more. "I am your brewmaster and I might be the mother of your child. I care about this baby and I could care very much for you—but not if you're going to spend the rest of our lives ordering me about. I am not your underling, Zeb. You don't get to decide that what you *think* you want is the same thing that I need. Because I'm only going to say this once. I'm sorry you had a miserable childhood. But it had nothing—not a damn thing—to do with the fact that you were raised by a single parent." A tear trickled down the side of her face and she scrubbed it away. "Don't you dare act like you're the only one raised by a single parent who had to work and sacrifice to survive."

"I never said that." But too late, he remembered her telling him how her mother had died in a car accident when she was two.

"Didn't you?" She moved in closer, and for a delusional second, he thought all was forgiven when she leaned in to kiss his cheek. But then she stepped back. "I give a damn, Zeb. Never think I don't. But I won't let your fears dictate my life."

She stepped around him, and this time, he didn't pull her back. He couldn't. Because he had the awful feeling that she might be right.

The door shut behind her, but he just stood there. Numbly, he looked down at the diamond ring in his hand. His father wouldn't have committed to the rest of his life with a woman he had gotten pregnant—he knew that.

But everything else?

He knew so little and the thing was, he wasn't sure he wanted to know more. He didn't know exactly what had happened between his parents. He couldn't be sure what made his mother the most bitter—the fact that Hardwick Beaumont had cast her aside? Or had it been something else? Had he forced her out of the company? Made her leave town and go back to Atlanta?

Why was this even a question? Hardwick had been married to a wealthy and powerful woman in her own right. Zeb was only four months younger than Chadwick. Of course Hardwick would've done everything within his power to hide Emily and Zeb.

And Zeb's mother…had she resented him? He was a living reminder of her great mistake—undeniable with his father's green eyes. Maybe she hadn't been able to love Zeb enough. And maybe—just maybe—that wasn't his fault.

# Fourteen

She couldn't do this. Hell, at this point, she wasn't even sure what "this" was.

Could she be with Zeb? Could they have a relationship? Or would it always devolve into awful awkwardness? Could she work with him or was that impossible? If she didn't work at the brewery, what was she going to do?

It was hard enough to be a woman and a brewmaster. It wasn't like there were tons of jobs ripe for the picking at breweries conveniently located near her apartment. Plus, she was kind of pregnant. How was she supposed to interview at companies that might or might not exist and then ask for maternity leave after only a month or two on the job?

The entire situation was ridiculous. And she couldn't even think the whole thing over while drinking a bottle of beer. Somehow, that was the straw that was going to break her back. How was she going to brew beer without testing it?

There was a possible solution—she could go to Chadwick. He'd find a place for her at Percheron Drafts, she was pretty sure. And at least in the past, he had demonstrated a willingness to work around maternity leave. He knew what she was capable of, and frankly, his was the only brewery within the area that wouldn't force her to relocate. Plus…her child would be a Beaumont. Sort of. Chadwick would be her baby's uncle and the man was nothing if not loyal to the family name.

But even just thinking about going to Chadwick felt wrong. She wasn't six, running to her father to tattle. She was a grown woman. She'd gotten herself into this mess and she had to get herself out of it.

The worst part was, Zeb had been right. There *was* something between them. There had been since the very first moment she had walked into his office and locked eyes with him. There was chemistry and raw sexual attraction and the sex was amazing. And when he was doing everything right, he was practically…perfect.

But when he wasn't perfect, he *really* wasn't perfect.

Instead of going back to her apartment, Casey found herself heading toward her father's small ranch house in Brentwood. She'd grown up in this little house, and at one time, it had seemed like a mansion to her. She hadn't ever wanted to live in a real mansion. She didn't need to be surrounded by all the trappings of luxury—and she also did not need a diamond that probably cost more than a year's salary on her finger.

Instead, she wanted what she'd had growing up. A father who doted on her, who taught her how to do things like change a tire and throw a baseball and brew beer. A father who protected her.

She hadn't grown up with all the luxuries that money could buy. But she'd been happy. Was it wrong to want that? Was it wrong to *demand* that?

No. It wasn't. So that wasn't the right question.

The bigger question was, could she demand that of Zeb?

She was happy to see that the lights were on at home. Sometimes a girl needed her father. She walked in the house, feeling a little bit like a teenager who had stayed out past curfew and was about to get in trouble. "Daddy?"

"In the kitchen," he called back.

Casey smiled at that. Any other parent who was in the kitchen might reasonably be expected to be cooking. But not Carl Johnson. She knew without even seeing it that he had something taken apart on the kitchen table—a lamp or doorbell, something.

True to form, a chandelier was sitting in the middle of the table, wires strung everywhere.

The chandelier was a piece of work—cut crystal prisms caught the light and made it look like the room was glowing. It belonged in a mansion like Zeb's. Here, in her father's house, it looked horribly out of place. She knew the feeling.

It was such a comforting thing, sitting at this table while her father tinkered with this or that. Casey slid into her old seat. "How are you doing, Daddy?"

"Pretty good. How are you?" He looked at her and paused. "Honey? Is everything okay?"

*No.* Things were not all right and she wasn't sure how to fix them. "I think I've made a mistake."

He rested his hand on her shoulder. "Are you in trouble? You know I don't like you living in that apartment by yourself. There's still plenty of room for you here."

She smiled weakly at him. "It's not that. But I… I did something stupid and now I think I've messed everything up."

"Does this have something to do with work?" When Casey didn't reply immediately, her dad pressed on. "This is about your new boss?"

There was no good way to say this. "Yeah, it does. I'm… I'm pregnant."

Her father stiffened, his grip on her shoulder tight before he quickly released her. "Them Beaumonts— I never did trust them. Are you okay? Did he hurt you?"

Casey slumped forward, head in her hands and her elbows on the table. "No, it's not like that, Dad. I *like* him. He likes me. But I'm not sure that that's going to be enough." She looked at her father. He looked skeptical. "He asked me to marry him."

Her father sat straight up. "He did? Well, I guess that's the right thing to do—better than what his old man would've done." There was a long pause during which Casey went back to slumping against her hands. "Do you want to get married? Because you don't have to do anything you don't want to, honey."

"I don't know what to do. When he asked me, he made it clear that he expected me to quit my job and stay home and be a mother full-time." She sighed. It wasn't only that, though.

No, the thing that really bothered her had been the implication that she, Casey Johnson, wasn't good enough to be the mother to his child as she was. Instead, she needed to become someone else. The perfect mother. And what the hell did she know about mothering? Nothing. She'd never had one.

"And that's not what I want. I fought hard to get my job, Dad. And I like brewing beer. I don't want to throw that all away because of one mistake. But if I don't marry him, how am I going to keep working at the brewery?" Her father opened his mouth, but she cut him off. "And no, I don't think asking Chadwick for a job is the best solution, either. I have no desire to be the rope in Beaumont tug-of-war."

They sat quietly for a few moments, but it wasn't long until her father had picked up a few pieces of wire. He began stripping them in an absentminded sort of way. "This guy—"

"Zeb. Zeb Richards."

Another piece of copper shone in the light. "This Zeb—he's one of them Beaumont bastards, right?" Casey nodded. "And he offered to marry you so his kid wouldn't be a bastard like he was?"

"Yeah. I just… I just don't want that to be the only reason. I mean, I can see he's trying to do the right thing, but if I get married, I'd kind of like it to be for love."

Her dad nodded and continued to strip the wire. "I wish your mom were here," he said in an offhand way. "I don't know what to tell you, honey. But I will say this. Your mom and I got married because we had to."

"What?" Casey shot straight up in her chair and stared at him. Her father was blushing. Oh, *Lord*.

"I never told you about this, because it didn't seem right. We'd been dating around and she got pregnant and I asked her to marry me. I hadn't before then, because I wasn't sure I wanted to settle down, but with you on the way, I grew up—fast."

She gaped at him. "I had no idea, Dad."

"I didn't want you to think you were a mistake, honey. Because you are the best thing that's ever happened to me." His eyes shone and he cleared his throat a few times—all while still stripping wire. "Anyway, that first year—that was rough. We had to learn how to talk to each other, how to live together.

But you were born, and suddenly, everything about us just made more sense. And then when the accident came…" He shuddered. "The reason I'm telling you this," he went on in a more serious voice, as if he hadn't just announced that she was a surprise, "is that sometimes love comes a little later. If you guys like each other and you both want this kid, maybe you should think about it." He put down his wire trimmers and rested a hand on hers. "The most important thing is that you two talk to each other."

She felt awful because, well, there hadn't been a lot of talk. She'd gone over to his place tonight to do just that, and instead, they'd fallen into bed.

The one time she had sat down and had a conversation with the man had been at the ball game. She had liked him a great deal then—more than enough to bring him home with her. Maybe they could make this work.

No matter what Zeb had said, they didn't have to get married. Times had changed and her dad wasn't about to bust out a shotgun to escort them down the aisle.

She wasn't opposed to getting married. She didn't have anything against marriage. She just… Well, she didn't want their marriage to be on his terms only.

She knew who she was. She was a woman in her early thirties, unexpectedly pregnant. But she was also a huge sports fan. She could rewire a house. She brewed beer and changed her own oil.

She was never going to be a perfect stay-at-home

mom, baking cookies and wearing pearls and lunching with ladies. That wasn't who she was.

If Zeb wanted to marry her and raise their child as a family, then not only did he have to accept that she was going to do things differently, but he was going to have to support her. Encourage her.

That did not mean taking her job away under the pretext of taking care of her. That meant helping her find a way to work at the job she loved *and* raise a happy, healthy child.

She wanted it all.

And by God, it was all or nothing.

But men—even men as powerful as Zebadiah Richards—were not mind readers. She knew that. Hell, she was *living* that.

She needed to tell him what she wanted. Without falling into bed with him and without it devolving into awkward awfulness.

"I sure am sorry, honey," her dad went on. "I'd love to be a grandfather—but I hate that this has put you in an awkward position." He gave her fingers a squeeze. "You know that, no matter what you decide, I'll be here to back you up."

She leaned in to her dad's shoulder and he wrapped his arms around her and hugged her. "I know, Daddy. I appreciate it."

"Tell you what," Dad said when she straightened up. "Tomorrow's Friday, right? And the Rockies play a game at three. Why don't you play hooky tomorrow? Stay here with me tonight. We'll make a day of it."

She knew that this was not a solution in any way, shape or form. At some point, she was going to have to sit down with Zeb and hash out what, exactly, they were going to do.

Soon. Next week, she'd be an adult again. She would deal with this unexpected pregnancy with maturity and wisdom. Eventually, she needed to talk with Zeb.

But for right now, she needed to be the girl she'd always been.

Sometimes, fathers did know best.

# Fifteen

"Where is she?"

The man Zeb had stopped—middle-aged, pot-bellied… He knew that he'd been introduced to this man before. Larry? Lance? Something like that. It wasn't important.

What was important was finding Casey.

"She's not here," the man said, his chins wobbling dangerously.

Zeb supposed he should be thankful that, since Casey was one of exactly two women in the production department, everyone knew which "she" he was talking about.

"Yes, I can see that. What I want to know," he said

slowly and carefully, which caused all the blood to drain out of the guy's face, "is where she is now."

It wasn't fair to terrorize employees like this, but dammit, Zeb needed to talk to Casey. She had stormed out of his house last night and by the time he'd gotten dressed, she had disappeared. She hadn't been at her apartment—the security guy said he hadn't seen her. In desperation, Zeb had even stopped by the brewery, just to make sure she wasn't tinkering with her brews. But the place had been quiet and the night shift swore she hadn't been in.

Her office was just as dark this morning. He didn't know where she was and he was past worrying and headed straight for full-on panic.

Which meant that he was currently scaring the hell out of one of his employees. He stared at the man, willing himself not to shake the guy. "Well?"

"She said she wouldn't be in today."

Zeb took a deep breath and forced himself to remain calm. "Do you have any idea where she might be?"

He must not have been doing a good job at the whole "calm" thing, because his employee backed up another step. "Sometimes she takes off in the afternoon to go to a game. With her dad. But you wouldn't fire her for that, right?" The man straightened his shoulders and approximated a stern look. "I don't think you should."

*The game.* Of course—why hadn't Zeb thought of that? She had season tickets, right? She'd be at the game. The relief was so strong it almost buckled his knees.

"No, I'm not going to fire her," he assured the guy. "Thanks for the tip, though. And keep up the good work."

On the walk back to his office, he called up the time for the baseball game. Three o'clock—that wasn't her taking the afternoon off. That was her taking the whole day. Had he upset her so much that she couldn't even face him? It wasn't like her to avoid a confrontation, after all.

What a mess. His attempt at a marriage proposal last night had not been his best work. But then, he had no experience proposing marriage while his brain was still fogged over from an amazing climax. He didn't have any experience in proposing marriage at all.

That was the situation he was going to change, though. He couldn't walk away from her. Hell, he hadn't even been able to do that before she had realized she was pregnant. There was something about her that he couldn't ignore. Yes, she was beautiful, and yes, she challenged him. Boy, did she challenge him. But there was more to it than that.

His entire life had been spent trying to prove that he was someone. That he was a Beaumont, that he belonged in the business world—that he mattered, regardless of his humble origins or the color of his skin.

And for all that Casey argued with him, she never

once asked him to be anyone other than himself. She accepted him as who he was—even if who he was happened to be a man who sometimes said the wrong thing at the wrong time.

He had made her a promise that he would take care of her, and by God, he was going to do that.

But this time, he was going to ask her how she wanted him to take care of her. Because he should have known that telling her what to do was a bad idea.

Ah, the seats behind hers were still available for this afternoon's game. Zeb bought the tickets.

He was going to do something he had never done before—he was going to take the afternoon off work.

"You want me to go get you some more nachos, honey?" Dad asked for the third time in a mere two innings.

Casey looked down at the chips covered in gloppy cheese. She was only kind of pregnant—wasn't it too soon for her stomach to be doing this many flips?

"I'm okay." She looked up and saw Dad staring at her. He looked so eager that she knew he needed something to do. "Really. But I could use another Sprite." Frankly, at this point, clear soda was the only thing keeping her stomach settled.

"I'll be right back," Dad said with a relieved smile, as if her problems could all be solved with more food. *Men*, Casey thought with another grin after he was gone.

Whereas she had no idea what she could do to make this better. No, it wasn't the most mature thing in the world to have skipped work today. It was just delaying the inevitable conversation that she would have to have with Zeb at some point or another.

There had been a moment last night—the moment before the kiss—where he'd told her that he was going to take care of her. That had been what she wanted. Hadn't that been why she'd gone to her dad after she had stormed out of Zeb's house? Because she wanted someone to take care of her?

But it wasn't a fair comparison. Her father had known her for her entire life. Of course he would know what she wanted—wasn't that why they were at this game today? It wasn't fair for her to hope and hope and just keep on hoping, dammit, that Zeb would guess correctly. Especially not when he'd gotten so close. There *was* a big part of her that wanted him to take care of her.

There was an equally big part of her that did not want to quit her job and be a stay-at-home mom. What if he couldn't see that? He was a hard-driving businessman who wasn't used to taking no for an answer. What if she couldn't convince him that she would be a better mom if she could keep her job and keep doing what she loved?

She was keeping her eye on the ball when she heard someone shuffling into the seat behind her. By instinct, she leaned forward to avoid any accidental hot dogs down the back of her neck. But as she did so, she startled as a voice came low and close to her ear. "It's a nice afternoon for baseball, isn't it?"

*Zeb.* She would recognize his voice anywhere—deep and serious, with just a hint of playfulness around the edge.

"Nice enough to skip work, even," he added when she didn't manage to come up with a coherent response.

Okay, now he was teasing her. She settled back in her chair, but she didn't turn around and look at him. She didn't want to see him in the suit and she didn't want to see him in a T-shirt. So she kept her eyes focused on the game in front of her. "How did you find me?"

"I asked Larry. I should've figured it out by myself. You weren't at your apartment and you weren't at work."

"I went home—I mean, my dad's home."

"I upset you. I didn't mean to, but I did." He exhaled and she felt his warmth against the back of her neck. "I shouldn't have assumed you would want to stay home. I know you and I know you're far too ambitious to give up everything you've worked for just because of something like this."

Now she did twist around. Good Lord—he was wearing purple. A Rockies T-shirt and a Rockies hat.

"You blend," she said in surprise. "I didn't think you knew how to do that."

"I can be taught." One corner of his mouth curved up in a small smile—the kind of smile that sent a shiver down her back. "I'm working on doing a better job of listening."

"Really?"

"Really. I have to tell you, I was frantic this morning when I couldn't find you at work. I was afraid you might quit on me and then where would I be?"

"But that's a problem, don't you see? How am I going to do my job? How am I going to brew beer if I can't drink it?"

Zeb settled back in his seat, that half smile still firmly on his face. "One of the things I've learned during my tenure as CEO of the Beaumont Brewery is that my employees do not drink on the job. They may sample in small quantities, but no one is ever drunk while they're at work—a fact which I appreciate. And I've also learned that I have extremely competent employees who care deeply about our brewery."

She stared at him in confusion. "What are you saying?"

He had the nerve to shrug nonchalantly. "I grew up in a hair salon, listening to women talk about pregnancies and babies and children. Obviously, we have to check with a doctor, but I think you taking a small sip every now and then isn't going to hurt anyone. And I don't want that to be the reason why you think you would have to leave a job you love."

She began to get a crick in her lower back. "Why are you here?" Because he was being perfect again and when he was perfect, he was simply irresistible.

"I'm here for you, Casey. I screwed up last night—I didn't ask you what you wanted. So that's what I'm doing now. What do you want to do?"

She was only vaguely aware that she was staring at him, mouth wide-open. But this was *the* moment. If she didn't tell him what she wanted right now, she might never get another chance.

"Come sit by me," she said. Obligingly, Zeb clambered down over the back of Dad's seat and settled in.

For a moment, Casey was silent as she watched the batter line out to right field. Zeb didn't say anything, though. He just waited for her.

"Okay," she said, mentally psyching herself up for this. Why could she defend her beer and her employees—but asking something for herself was such a struggle?

Well, to hell with that. She was doing this. Right now. "It's hard for me to ask for stuff that I want," she admitted. It wasn't a graceful statement, but it was the truth.

Zeb turned and looked at her funny. "You? Didn't you barge into my office and tell me off on my first day?"

"It's different. I defend my job and I defend my workers but for me to sit here and tell you what I want—it's…it's hard, okay? So just humor me."

"I will always listen to you, Casey. I want you to know that."

Her cheeks began to heat and the back of her neck prickled, but she wasn't allowing herself to get lost in the awkwardness of the moment. Instead, she forged ahead.

"The last time we were at a game together… I wanted you to tell me that I was beautiful and sensual and…and gorgeous. But it felt stupid, asking for that, so I didn't, and then after we…" She cleared her throat, hoping against hope that she hadn't turned bright red and knowing it was way too late for that. "Well, afterward, what you said made me feel even less pretty than normal. And so I shut down on you."

Now it was his turn to stare at her, mouth open and eyes wide. "But…do you have any idea how much you turn me on? How gorgeous you are?"

God, she was going to die of embarrassment. "It's not that—okay, maybe it is. But it's that I've always been this tomboy. And when we were together in my kitchen, it was good. Great," she added quickly when he notched an eyebrow at her. "But I don't want that to be all there is. If we're going to have a relationship, I need romance. And most people think I don't, because I drink beer and I watch ball games."

She had not died of mortification yet, which had to count for something.

"Romance," he said, but he didn't sound like he was mocking her. Instead, he sounded…thoughtful.

A small flicker of hope sparked to life underneath the heat of embarrassment. "Yes."

He touched her then, his hand on hers. More heat. There'd always be this heat between them. "Duly noted. What else? Because I will do everything in my power to give you what you want and what you need."

For a moment, she almost got lost in his gaze. God, those green eyes—from the very first moment, they had pulled her in and refused to let her go. "I don't want to give up my job. And I don't want to quit and go someplace else. I've worked hard for my job and I love it. I love everything about making beer and everything about working for the brewery. Even my new CEO, who occasionally sends out mixed signals."

At that, Zeb laughed out loud. "Can you keep a secret?"

"Depends on the secret," she said archly.

"Before I met you, I don't think I ever did anything but work. That's all I've known. It's all my mom did and I thought I had to prove myself to her, to my father—to everyone. I've been so focused on being the boss and on besting the Beaumonts for so long that…" He sighed and looked out at the game. But Casey could tell he wasn't seeing it. "That I've forgotten how to be me. Then I met you. When I'm with you, I don't feel like I have to be something that I'm not. I don't have to prove myself over and over again. I can just be *me*." The look he gave her was tinged with sadness. "It's hard for me to let go of that—of being the CEO. But you make me want to do better."

"Oh, Zeb—there's so much more to you than just this brewery."

He cupped her face. "That goes for you, too—you are more than just a brewmaster to me. You are a passionate, beautiful woman who earned my respect first and my love second."

Tears begin to prick at Casey's eyes. Stupid hormones. "Oh, Zeb…"

"There's something between us and I don't want to screw that up. Any more than I already have," he added, looking sheepish.

"What do you want?" She felt it was only fair to ask him.

"I want to know my child. I want to be a part of his or her life. I don't want my child to be raised as a bastard." He paused and Casey felt a twinge of disappointment. It wasn't like she could disagree with that kind of sentiment—it was a damn noble one.

But was it enough? She wanted to be wanted not just because she was pregnant but because she was… Well, because she was Casey.

But before she could open her mouth to tell Zeb this, he went on, "That's not all."

"It's not?" Her voice came out with a bit of a waver in it.

He leaned in closer. "It's not. I want to be with someone who I respect, who I trust to pull me back to myself when I've forgotten how to be anything but the boss. I want to be with someone who sparks something in me, someone I look forward to coming home to every single night." Casey gasped, but he kept going. "I want to be with someone who's just as committed to her work as I am to mine—but who also knows how to relax and kick back. I want to be with someone who understands the different families I'm a part of now and who loves me because of them, not in spite of them." His lips were now just a breath away from hers. She could feel his warmth and she wanted nothing more than to melt into him again. "But most of all, I want to be with someone who can tell me what she wants—what she needs—and when she needs it. So tell me, Casey—what do you want?"

This was really happening. "I want to know you care, that you'll fight for me and the baby—and for us. That you'll protect us and support us, even if we do things that other people don't think we should."

Oh, God—that grin on him was too much. She couldn't resist him and she was tired of trying. "Like be the youngest female brewmaster in the country?"

He understood. "Yeah, that. If we do this, I want to do this right," she told him. "But I want to meet you in the middle. I don't know if I want to live in the big house and I know we can't live in my tiny apartment."

His eyes warmed. "We can talk about that."

"That's what I want—I want to know that I can talk to you and know that you'll listen. I want to know that everything is going to work out for the best."

He pulled back, just the tiniest bit. "I can't guarantee anything, Casey. But I can promise you this—I will love you and our baby no matter what."

Love. That was the something between them—the thing that neither of them could walk away from.

"That's what I want," she told him. She leaned into him, wrapping her hand around the back of his neck and pulling him in closer. "I love you, too. That's all."

"Then I'm yours. All you have to do is ask." He gave her a crooked grin. "I won't always get it right. I'm not a mind reader, you know."

She couldn't help it—she laughed. "Did the all-powerful Zebadiah Richards just admit there was something he couldn't do?"

"Shh," he teased, his eyes sparkling. "Don't tell anyone. It's a secret." Then he leaned in closer. "Let me give you everything, Casey. We'll run the brewery together and raise our kid. We'll do it our way."

"*Yes.* I want you."

Just as his lips brushed against hers, she heard someone clearing his throat—loudly.

*Dad.* In all the talk, she'd forgotten that he'd left to fetch a soda for her. She jolted in her seat, but Zeb didn't let her go. Instead, he wrapped his arms around her shoulders.

"Everything okay?" Dad asked as he eyed the two of them suspiciously. "You want me to get rid of him, honey?"

Casey looked up at her dad as she leaned back into Zeb's arms and smiled. "Nope," she said, knowing that this was right. "I want him to stay right here with me."

Everything she'd ever wanted was hers—a family, her job and Zeb. He was all hers.

All she'd had to do was ask for him.

* * * * *

*Pick up all the* BEAUMONT HEIRS *novels
from Sarah M. Anderson!
One Colorado family, limitless scandal!
NOT THE BOSS'S BABY
TEMPTED BY A COWBOY
A BEAUMONT CHRISTMAS WEDDING
HIS SON, HER SECRET
FALLING FOR HER FAKE FIANCÉ
HIS ILLEGITIMATE HEIR
Available now from Harlequin Desire!*

*And don't miss CJ's story,
RICH RANCHER FOR CHRISTMAS
coming December 2016!*

***

*If you're on Twitter, tell us what you think
of Harlequin Desire! #harlequindesire*

## COMING NEXT MONTH FROM

HARLEQUIN®
*Desire*

### Available November 8, 2016

**#2479 HOLD ME, COWBOY**
*Copper Ridge* • by Maisey Yates
Rich-as-sin cowboy Sam McCormack wants nothing to do with ice princess
Madison West, but when they're snowed in together at a mountain retreat,
their red-hot attraction quickly burns through all their misconceptions...

**#2480 ONE HEIR...OR TWO?**
*Billionaires and Babies* • by Yvonne Lindsay
As promised, Kayla became the surrogate mother for her late sister's
baby—and she's expecting again! But when complications arise, the only
person who can help is the sexy billionaire donor who doesn't yet know
he's a dad...

**#2481 HIS SECRETARY'S LITTLE SECRET**
*The Lourdes Brothers of Key Largo* • by Catherine Mann
Organizing Easton Lourdes's workaholic life is a full-time job, and
secretary Portia Soto is the best at keeping things professional. But
when a hurricane sends her into her boss's arms—and his bed—the
consequences will change everything...

**#2482 HOLIDAY BABY SCANDAL**
*Mafia Moguls* • by Jules Bennett
Dangerous Ryker Barrett owes the O'Shea family everything—and he
proves his loyalty by keeping his hands off Laney O'Shea. Until he not only
seduces her, but gets her pregnant, too! Will his dark past keep him from
forever with her?

**#2483 HIS PREGNANT CHRISTMAS BRIDE**
*The Billionaires of Black Castle* • by Olivia Gates
Ivan left the woman he loved once, to protect them both. But when
he saves her from an attack, he can no longer stay away. Will keeping
Anastasia as his bride mean overcoming the sinister events that shaped
him?

**#2484 BACK IN THE ENEMY'S BED**
*Dynasties: The Newports* • by Michelle Celmer
Roman betrayed Grace years ago. So when the wealthy ex-soldier
swaggers back into her life, she's prepared to turn the tables on him. But
she can't resist the unexpected desire between them—even as his secrets
threaten to tear them apart...

---

**YOU CAN FIND MORE INFORMATION ON UPCOMING HARLEQUIN® TITLES,
FREE EXCERPTS AND MORE AT WWW.HARLEQUIN.COM.**

HDCNM1016

# REQUEST YOUR FREE BOOKS!
## 2 FREE NOVELS PLUS 2 FREE GIFTS!

**H HARLEQUIN®**

*Desire*

### ALWAYS POWERFUL, PASSIONATE AND PROVOCATIVE

**YES!** Please send me 2 FREE Harlequin® Desire novels and my 2 FREE gifts (gifts are worth about $10). After receiving them, if I don't wish to receive any more books, I can return the shipping statement marked "cancel." If I don't cancel, I will receive 6 brand-new novels every month and be billed just $4.55 per book in the U.S. or $5.24 per book in Canada. That's a savings of at least 13% off the cover price! It's quite a bargain! Shipping and handling is just 50¢ per book in the U.S. and 75¢ per book in Canada.* I understand that accepting the 2 free books and gifts places me under no obligation to buy anything. I can always return a shipment and cancel at any time. Even if I never buy another book, the two free books and gifts are mine to keep forever.

225/326 HDN GH2P

| | |
|---|---|
| Name | (PLEASE PRINT) |

| | |
|---|---|
| Address | Apt. # |

| | | |
|---|---|---|
| City | State/Prov. | Zip/Postal Code |

Signature (if under 18, a parent or guardian must sign)

### Mail to the **Reader Service:**
**IN U.S.A.:** P.O. Box 1867, Buffalo, NY 14240-1867
**IN CANADA:** P.O. Box 609, Fort Erie, Ontario L2A 5X3

**Want to try two free books from another line?**
**Call 1-800-873-8635 or visit www.ReaderService.com.**

* Terms and prices subject to change without notice. Prices do not include applicable taxes. Sales tax applicable in N.Y. Canadian residents will be charged applicable taxes. Offer not valid in Quebec. This offer is limited to one order per household. Not valid for current subscribers to Harlequin Desire books. All orders subject to credit approval. Credit or debit balances in a customer's account(s) may be offset by any other outstanding balance owed by or to the customer. Please allow 4 to 6 weeks for delivery. Offer available while quantities last.

**Your Privacy**—The Reader Service is committed to protecting your privacy. Our Privacy Policy is available online at www.ReaderService.com or upon request from the Reader Service.

We make a portion of our mailing list available to reputable third parties that offer products we believe may interest you. If you prefer that we not exchange your name with third parties, or if you wish to clarify or modify your communication preferences, please visit us at www.ReaderService.com/consumerchoice or write to us at Reader Service Preference Service, P.O. Box 9062, Buffalo, NY 14240-9062. Include your complete name and address.

HD15

## SPECIAL EXCERPT FROM

### (H) HARLEQUIN®

# *Desire*

*Rich-as-sin cowboy Sam McCormack wants nothing
to do with ice princess Madison West, but when
they're snowed in together at a mountain retreat,
their red-hot attraction quickly burns through all their
misconceptions…*

*Read on for a sneak peek of*
**HOLD ME, COWBOY**
*the latest in Maisey Yates's* New York Times *bestselling*
**COPPER RIDGE** *series!*

"Are you going to suggest that I need *you*?" she asked,
her voice choked.

Lightning streaked through his blood, and in that
moment, he was lost. It didn't matter that he thought
she was insufferable, a prissy little princess who didn't
appreciate anything she had. It didn't matter that he was
up here to work.

All that mattered was he hadn't touched a woman in a
long time, and Madison West was so close all he would
have to do was shift his weight slightly and he'd be able
to take her into his arms.

"Well," he said, "you have a couple of the essential
ingredients to have yourself a pretty fun evening. All you
seem to be missing is a good man. I'm not very nice,
Madison," he said, leaning in, "but I could damn sure
show you a good time."

She should throw him out. She looked over at him, and her libido made a dash to the foreground. That was the problem. He irritated her. He was exactly the kind of man she didn't like. He was cocky; he was rough and crude. However, there was something about the way he looked in a tight T-shirt that made a mockery of all that very certain hatred.

"Are you going to take off your coat and stay awhile?" That question, asked in a faintly mocking tone, sent a dart of tension straight down between her thighs.

She could *not* take off her coat. Because she was wearing nothing more than a little scrap of red lace underneath it. And now it was all she could think of. "It's cold," she snapped. "Maybe if you went to work getting the electricity back on rather than standing here making terrible double entendres I would be able to take off my coat."

The maddening man raised his eyebrows, shooting her a look that clearly said Suit yourself, then set about looking for the fuse box. She let out an exasperated sigh and followed his path, stopping when she saw him leaning against the wall, a little metal door between the logs open as he examined the switches inside.

"It's not a fuse. That means there's something else going on." He slammed the door shut and turned back to look at her. "You should come over to my cabin."

*Don't miss*
*HOLD ME, COWBOY*
*by* New York Times *bestselling author Maisey Yates,*
*available November 2016 wherever*
*Harlequin® Desire books and ebooks are sold.*

www.Harlequin.com

Copyright © 2016 by Maisey Yates

HDEXP1016R

# Whatever You're Into… Passionate Reads

Looking for more passionate reads from Harlequin®?
Fear not! Harlequin® Presents, Harlequin® Desire and
Harlequin® Blaze offer you irresistible romance stories
featuring powerful heroes.

## ⬥HARLEQUIN *Presents.*

Do you want alpha males, decadent glamour and jet-set
lifestyles? Step into the sensational, sophisticated world of
Harlequin® Presents, where sinfully tempting heroes ignite a
fierce and wickedly irresistible passion!

## ⬥HARLEQUIN *Desire*

Harlequin® Desire novels are powerful, passionate and
provocative contemporary romances set against a backdrop of
wealth, privilege and sweeping family saga. Alpha heroes with
a soft side meet strong-willed but vulnerable heroines amid a
dramatic world of divided loyalties, high-stakes conflict and
intense emotion.

## ⬥HARLEQUIN *Blaze*

Harlequin® Blaze stories sizzle with strong heroines and
irresistible heroes playing the game of modern love and lust.
They're fun, sexy and always steamy.

Be sure to check out our full selection of books
within each series every month!

www.Harlequin.com

HPASSION2016

Turn your love of reading into rewards you'll love with

# Harlequin My Rewards

**Join for FREE today at
www.HarlequinMyRewards.com**

Earn **FREE BOOKS** of your choice.

Experience **EXCLUSIVE OFFERS** and contests.

Enjoy **BOOK RECOMMENDATIONS**
selected just for you.

**PLUS!** Sign up now
and get **500** points
right away!

Earn
FREE
REWARDS
Join
Today!
HarlequinMyRewards.com

MYR16R